Roy Blakeley's Bee-line Hike

Percy Keese Fitzhugh

1

ROY BLAKELEY'S BEE-LINE HIKE

CHAPTER I

WE LOSE A MEMBER

Now I'm going to tell you about the bee-line hike. Maybe you'll say you don't believe everything I tell you about it, but one thing sure, it's a straight story. It wasn't so long, that hike, but—oh, boy!

Now the first thing I have to do in this story is to get rid of Charlie Seabury. That's easy. Then the next thing I have to do is to tell you about Pee-wee Harris. Gee whiz, I wish we could get rid of him. That kid belongs in the Raven Patrol and when those fellows went up to Temple Camp they wished him on us for the summer. They said it was a good turn. Can you beat that? I suppose we've got to take him up to camp with us when we go. Anyway the crowd up there will have some peace in the meantime, so we're doing a good turn, that's what I said.

So this story is just about my own patrol and Pee-wee Harris, and some buildings and a couple of valleys and a hill and some pie, and a forest and some ice cream cones and a big tree and a back yard and a woman and a ghost and a couple of girls and ten cents' worth of peanut brittle. It's about a college, too. Maybe you think we're not very smart on account of being kind of crazy, but anyway we went through college in ten minutes. So you can see from that how bright we are. That's why we call ourselves the Silver Foxes.

Now Charlie Seabury (he has seven merit badges) has a grandfather who lives out near the Mississippi and his grandfather asked him to go out there and spend the summer. No wonder they call that man grand.

Charlie came to me because I'm patrol leader, and he said, "Shall I go out there and spend the summer?"

I said, "Sure, you might as well. If you hang around here all you'll spend is nickels."

He said, "But when you start up for camp you'll want a full patrol, won't you? You can't count Pee-wee in the Silver Foxes."

"Talk of something pleasant," I told him. "You go ahead out west and leave the patrol to us. We'll find a new member and when you come back in the Fall you can start the new patrol that Mr. Ellsworth is always talking about."

He said, "Good idea; what shall we call it?"

"Call it the police patrol or whatever you want to, I don't care," I told him.

He said, "Well, I guess I'll go. My grandfather has a big apple orchard and everything, and I can go swimming in the Mississippi. I'll write to you."

"How is that going to get me any apples?" I asked him. "Go ahead, the sooner the quicker, and I'll have fewer Silver Foxes to worry about. Let your grandfather worry for a while."

So that's the end of Charlie Seabury in this story. We lost a scout and his grandfather lost an apple orchard. I should worry. Maybe, later, you'll hear about the Laughing Hyenas that he started. But believe me, there are laughs enough in this story without bothering our heads about that new outfit.

CHAPTER II

MISSIONARY WORK

We had about two weeks to hang around Bridgeboro (that's where we live) before starting for Temple Camp. If you want to know why we stayed behind when the Ravens and the Elks went, you'd better read the story that comes before this one. That will tell you how our young hero, the raving raven of the Ravens, happened to be wished on us, too.

Now a couple of days after Charlie Seabury started out west two or three of us were sitting in the swinging seat on my porch talking about what we'd do to kill time for a couple of weeks.

"What's the matter with killing Pee-wee?" Westy wanted to know.

I said, "Speak of angels and you'll hear the flutter of their wings; here he comes up the hill."

"What's he eating?" Dorry Benton asked.

"I think it's peanuts," Hunt Manners said.

Pretty soon the little angel eating peanuts crossed the road and cut up across the lawn. He's always cutting up in some way or other.

"For goodness' sake, look at him," I said; "he's a walking junk shop. We could sell him for old metal."

Honest, I had to laugh. That kid looked like a Christmas tree. He was wearing his belt-axe and it looked as if it weighed a ton the way it dragged his belt down. In front he had his scout jack-knife dangling from his belt and his big nickel-plated compass hanging by a cord around his neck. He had all his badges on, and besides he had his aluminum cooking set hanging by a strap from his shoulder. He had his brown scarf on too, he didn't care how hot it was. The reason the Ravens chose brown for their color is because they're all nuts in that patrol. He had his scout staff with the Raven pennant on it and he was jabbing it into the ground as he came along.

Westy said, "What's this? A traveling hardware store?"

Dorry said, "Are you starting off on a crusade, Kid? Where's your steel armor? What's the large idea? Have the Germans invaded Bridgeboro?"

I was laughing so hard I could hardly speak. The kid looked like that picture in the handbook that shows just how to wear the medals and things.

"What's this? A coffee-pot?" Ralph Warner asked him. "You must be going to join the Cook's Tours with all your cooking things. What's the big idea of all the exterior decorations?"

"I'm a delegation," Pee-wee said.

"A what?" I asked him.

"Don't you know what a missionary is?" he shot back at me.

"Good night! Pity the poor heathens," I said. "So that's what you've got the compass for! You're going to China? Break it to us gently. You sound like a Ford when you walk."

"You think you're smart, don't you?" he shouted. "I was out doing a good turn, so there. I was out doing a good turn for your patrol. I was trying to get you a new member. When you go after new members you've got to look like a scout, haven't you? You've got to show them what scouting is, so they'll see. Everybody knows that. Didn't you ever hear that it takes a scout to catch a scout?"

"You couldn't catch a snail with all that junk hanging on you," I told him. "Who did you try to catch?"

"Warde Hollister," he shouted.

Good night, we all began to laugh.

"Warde Hollister?" I said. "You couldn't catch that fellow with a lasso. He loves the wild and woolly front porch too much. You stand a tall chance of getting Warde Hollister into the scouts. You're wasting your time, Kiddo. What did he tell you?"

"He said he has something better to do with himself," Pee-wee said.

"There you go," Dorry told him; "that's him all over. Why should he join the Silver Foxes when he can shoot buffaloes and Indians and hunt train robbers and kidnap maidens and dig up buried treasure?"

"Where can he do that?" Pee-wee wanted to know.

"Right in the public library," I told him, "division B, second shelf from the top. That's a dangerous place, that is; I've known fellows to get killed in there. There used to be a kid that lived on Willow Place and he got drowned in a sea story in there."

"What are you talking about?" Pee-wee screamed. He always gets excited when we jolly him.

"We're talking about adventures," I said; "hair-breadth adventures—not even as wide as that, some of them. I know a fellow that got buried in a book; it was absorbing just like quicksand, and he got absorbed in it. What were you going to do, Kid? Throw the coffee-pot at him if he didn't join? You didn't intend to hack him to pieces with your scoutknife, did you? Because a scout is supposed to be kind."

"You make me tired, all of you!" Pee-wee shouted. "Do you want to hear about it or don't you?"

"Answered in the affirmative," I told him. "Begin at the end and go on till you come to the beginning."

"Then take the second turn to your left," Westy said.

"That's what I get for trying to do you a good turn," the kid shouted. "No wonder Warde Hollister said you were all crazy."

"Did he say that?" Westy wanted to know.

"Sure, and other people have said so, too," the kid piped up.

"They don't need to say so, we admit it," I told him. "Go ahead with your story. What do you want us to do? Light a camp-fire so you can unravel your yarn?"

"That fellow can be circum—circumnavigated yet," Pee-wee said, very dark and mysterious.

"Circumvented you mean," Westy said.

"You know what I mean," the kid shouted.

"Go ahead," I told him; "the plot grows thicker."

"Give us a couple of peanuts," Dorry said.

The kid turned his aluminum coffee-pot upside down and, good morning, sister Anne, it was full of peanuts!

"Let's see what's in the saucepan," I said.

CHAPTER III

A SOLEMN PLEDGE

So then we were all eating peanuts.

I said, "Go ahead, Kid, and tell us. You're a little brick to try to find us a new member. He didn't fall, hey?"

"He didn't even trip," Westy said.

"Keep still," I told him, "and let the kid tell us."

Pee-wee said, "I dressed all up and wore all my stuff so he'd see just what a scout is like. Because I thought maybe that would kind of lure him. I thought if he saw the cooking set it would remind him about camp-fires and eating and everything."

"What did he say?" Westy wanted to know.

"He said he had no use for scouts," the kid said. "He said they have to be all the time doing kind acts every day and that there isn't any fun playing soldiers. I told him there are different kinds of kind acts," the kid said. "I told him you don't have to be so awful kind. I told him it might be a kind act to break a window — if a house was on fire; that's what I told him. I told him he might do a good turn by throwing a lot of broken glass on the road to cut automobile tires — —"

"What kind of a good turn do you call that?" Dorry asked him. I was laughing so hard I couldn't speak.

"That's a new one on me," Ralph Warner said.

"Suppose there were bandits in the automobile?" the kid shouted. "There! You think you're so smart. I know lots of good turns that are fun. Suppose I tripped you up so you couldn't chase a — a — poor little girl so as to steal — a — a — —"

"A piece of candy from her," I said.

"That would be a good turn," the kid shouted.

I said, "Well, Kid, if a fellow doesn't believe in breaking windows and throwing broken glass in the street and tripping people up, he would never make much of a scout. I wouldn't want a fellow like that in my patrol. Forget it. We're just as much obliged to you, but the Public Library is the place for that wild animal. We could never tame him."

"Maybe if he could only see that scouts have a lot of fun," the kid said; "because he thinks they don't do anything but good turns. I wish I could get him for you, I know that, because you did a lot of things for me. But he only just laughed at me and he said we didn't have any fun."

I said, "Kid, you're a little brick. When it comes to good turns you eat them alive. We should worry about Warde Hollister. If he wants to camp out on his wild and woolly front porch, we should bother our young lives about him. Let him lurk in his hammock. Some day the rope will break and he'll die a horrible death. What are you squinting your eye at?" I asked Westy.

He was sitting on the swinging seat beside me squinting his eye awful funny.

He said, "Keep still, stop swinging for a second. Do you see that tree away, way over on the ridge? Do you know what kind of a tree that is?"

"It's a large tree," I said; "correct the first time. What about it?"

"It's a poplar tree," he said.

Dorry said, "All right, it's a large, popular tree. What about it?"

Westy said, "Take your hands off the swing, you fellows. I'm trying to get a bee-line on it. Do you know what I'd like to do?"

"Go down to Bennett's for ice cream cones?" I said.

"Come ahead!" Pee-wee shouted.

"You'd be arrested if you went on Main Street looking that way," I told him.

"Close one eye and look straight at that tree," Westy said. "Get right behind me. Now. Look."

"All right," I said, "I'm looking."

"Well, what's in a bee-line with that tree?" he asked me.

"A lot of stuff," I said; "buildings and things—and villages and landscapes."

"The line cuts Allison College right in half," Westy said. "See?"

"If it sliced a couple of slices off the High School that would be better," I said. "The High School just escapes. It crosses Main Street, I hope nobody trips over it."

"What do you mean? Trip over an imaginary line!" Pee-wee shouted at me.

"Sure," I said, "if you have a strong enough imagination. Oh, look where it goes right through Bennett's."

"Where?" the kid shouted. "Show me! Where?"

"Excuse me, I'm mistaken," I said. "It goes right—straight—wait a minute—it goes right straight through the dentist's—Dr. Wade's——"

"You make me tired!" Pee-wee yelled.

"Do you know what I'd like to do?" Westy said. "I'd like to start from here and go straight for that tree. A bee-line hike, that's what I'd call it. Let's see your compass, Kid. That tree is—just—wait a minute, hold still—that tree is just exactly—west. I'd like to start and hike right straight for it."

"How about buildings?" Hunt Manners wanted to know.

"If we came to buildings we'd have to go through them," Westy said. "Through them or over them. Or under them. Or else we'd have to move them out of the way. We'd make a solemn vow that we wouldn't turn to the right or left for anybody or anything. We'd hike right straight for that tree. What do you say?"

Oh, boy, you should have heard those fellows shout. That shows how crazy we are.

I said, "Carried by a large minority. All those who are unanimously in favor of a bee-line hike, eat another peanut. Settled. When shall we start? To-morrow morning? Righto!"

"No matter what happens we'll go right straight west," Dorry said.

"For the tree," Hunt Manners shouted.

"Even if we have to go a little — —" the kid started.

"No, you don't," I said. "We go straight through the dentist's."

"If things get in our way we'll use resources, hey?" he piped up.

"We'll use dynamite," I said. "Scouts of the Silver Fox Patrol and Pee-wee Harris, First Bridgeboro, New Jersey, Troop B. S. A., all gather around your patrol leader and each give him six peanuts as a token of loyalty. That's the way the knights used to do in history — —"

"It's a cinch being a patrol leader," Dorry said.

"Keep still," I told him, "and give me two more peanuts. Do you think I don't know how to count? Now all raise your hands and stick your thumbs in your ears while I say the vow. Ready? Go:

"Before the sun sinks in the sink to-morrow night, we, the members of the sterling silver triple-plated Fox Patrol will plant our patrol emblem under the branches of yonder popular tree, having taken a course due west from this swing seat on my porch, and turned neither to right nor left on the way even if we have to go through school again — —"

"Even if we have to go through the mathematics room," Dorry shouted.

"And hereby we pledge ourselves with ten more peanuts each to our gallant patrol leader — —"

"Have a heart," Westy said; "what is this? A hike or a monopoly?"

"It's a go," I said. "Nothing will stop us now. The world must be made safe for the Boy Scouts of America! Give me another peanut, somebody. Food will win the war. Hurrah, for the Silver-plated Fox Patrol and the bee-line hike!"

CHAPTER IV
WE START

Now I'll have to tell you about where I live and about Bridgeboro and all that, so you'll know the country we invaded. But you needn't think I'm going to bother you with geography because, gee whiz, I have no use for that. Believe me, when you see my picture on the cover of a book you'll know there is no history or geography or anything like that in it. And the only figures you'll see are the numbers of the pages, because I should worry about figures in vacation.

But anyway it's dandy up where I live. My father owns a lot of property up there and so everybody calls it Blakeley's hill. It's in Bridgeboro but kind of just outside ofBridgeboro—you know what I mean.

Maybe you know how it is with towns that have rivers running through them. Rivers run through valleys—that shows how smart I am. There is always high land on both sides of a river. I don't mean it has to be right close to the river.

Now this is the way it is where I live. Blakeley's hill isn't a hill exactly, it's a ridge. It runs along the same way the river runs. The state road runs along that ridge and our house is on the state road only it's way back from the road. We've got a dandy grapevine. We've got a sun parlor, too. That's where Mr. Blakeley's son sits and reads on rainy days. That's why we call it a sun parlor.

Now if you sit on our porch you can look down over Bridgeboro; you get a peach of a view. Beyond Bridgeboro you can see the river. That's where the town ends—at the river. There are a lot of turtles in that river. Across the river the land is low until you come to the other ridge. Now the space between the two ridges is the valley of the river. Correct, be seated.

In that low land between the river and the other ridge is Little Valley; that's a village. It's where Harry Donnelle lives. He's got a Cadillac, that fellow has. Lots of times he treats us to soda, but he won't be a scoutmaster. Oh, boy, but he'd make a dandy one. Little Valley isn't very big; it hasn't got its eyes open yet.

When you get past Little Valley there's a kind of a small hill and then you come to the ridge. Up on top of the ridge is that big tree that Westy was squinting at. There are a lot of other trees up there but that one is bigger than any of them. Anywhere between my house and that other ridge you can see that tree. Down in Bridgeboro maybe there are places where you can't see it on account of buildings, but most always you can see it. If you could have a string from my porch to that tree, the string would be right over Bridgeboro and the river and Little Valley and that other small hill. So now you know just how it is. From my porch to that tree is about seven miles as the crow flies, and believe me the crows have it easy compared to the boy scouts.

So now our troubles begin. If you want to follow us, all right, it's up to you. I should worry. We have troubles of our own.

The next morning we started from my porch. We reminded ourselves of the Pilgrims and Christopher Columbus and a lot of other people you meet in school. Our young hero, P. Harris, was all decorated up like a band wagon, belt-axe, badges, compass, cooking set, a big coil of rope and the horn part of a phonograph. He had that hanging over his back like a soldier's pack. The only thing he forgot to bring was the player piano from his house.

"What's that phonograph horn for?" Westy asked him.

"It's to use as a megaphone," he said. "Suppose we want to — to — shout for a — —"

"House to get out of the way?" I said.

"You never can tell when we may want to use it," he said.

"I'm sorry I didn't bring my mother's sewing machine along," Dorry said.

"We don't need that with this kid along," I said. "We'll have enough stitches in our sides from laughing."

"We ought to have some mothers and sweethearts and things to weep when we start off," the kid said.

I said, "I don't believe I've got any sweethearts around the house just at present, but wait a minute and I'll see."

"Tell them to bring some handkerchiefs," Westy said.

"And a couple of buckets of tears," Hunt Manners piped up.

I went inside and called to my mother and my sister Marjorie and asked them if they could come out on the porch and weep. My mother said she was very busy but she'd come and weep for about a minute. When they came out they were crying—from laughing so hard.

Then I delivered a speech. I said to my mother and sister, "You're supposed to keep on weeping and wringing your hands while I make a farewell speech. Don't you know the way the wives and sweethearts did when the Pilgrim Fathers started away?"

Then I said:

"Scouts of the Silver Fox Patrol and also the raving Raven that we have wished on us, there must be no good turns on this hike. We're going the same way the crow flies, only different. The first time we have to turn to right or left we will have to admit we're beaten, and come home. We'll have to turn back like somebody or other who started for some place once upon a time in the third grade history—an explorer. The battle cry is 'ONWARD.' If we do any good turns they'll have to be up and down, not to right or left. Anybody that wants to stay home can do it. At five o'clock this afternoon we intend to plant the Silver Fox emblem under that big poplar tree on west ridge. We'll start a fire there so all the world can see. That fire will mean triumph. It will mean we went in a bee-line. If we have to push Little Valley out of the way we'll do it—it isn't so big. We'll cross the valley——"

My mother said, "You'd better wear your rubbers."

I said, "Do you think Christopher Columbus and Henry Hudson wore rubbers? At five o'clock this afternoon you look over to west ridge and see what you see. We intend to go straight—it says in the handbook a scout lives straight—but we can beat that, we can go straight. We are going to go in a bee-line for that tree and take possession of it in the name of the Silver Fox Patrol B. S. A. This is the only real boy scout drive that ever happened—all others are imitations. This is the famous bee-line hike invented by Westy Martin. We're off!"

So then we raised our banner and started out. It was a big piece of cardboard fixed onto a scout staff and on it was printed with shoe-blacking:

THE BEE-LINE HIKE OF THE

SILVER FOX PATROL. GET

FROM UNDER, EVERYBODY

AND EVERYTHING.

Our first mishap was at the end of my lawn, when Pee-wee's garter broke and a lot of junk fell on the ground when he stooped down to fix it.

"Got a safety-pin?" he wanted to know.

I said, "Pick up your coffee-pot and things and put them in the megaphone and come ahead. Do you think we're going to start out to conquer the world with safety-pins?"

CHAPTER V
A STUMBLING BLOCK

Little we thought that inside of an hour we'd be on the road to fame. I don't mean that we turned to the right or left to get into the road. We just kind of bunked into fame. That hike was only seven miles long but in one way it went all the way out to the Pacific coast. Maybe it's in China by this time for all I know.

While we were going down the hill to get into Bridgeboro, Pee-wee said, "We ought to look kind of invincible, like conquerors."

I said, "Well, as long as you're the official junk wagon you might as well carry the standard."

"The what?" he wanted to know.

"The standard," I said; "that's Latin for banner. Didn't you ever hear of the Standard Oil Company?"

So we gave him the banner, and oh, boy, that kid did look funny, holding it up. He was scowling as if he thought he could frighten buildings out of the way. The stuff he had inside of his patented megaphone kept rattling and he sounded like a junk dealers' convention as he tramped along.

We decided that it would be best to go into regular formation so as to look more invincible and scare the civilized civilians in Bridgeboro.

"We'll strike terror, hey?" the kid said.

"I hope we strike a restaurant," Hunt Manners spoke up.

"I don't care what we strike as long as we don't strike our colors," I told him. "Suppose three fellows walk together, and three others behind them, and Pee-wee and I will walk ahead because I'm the leader and he's the standard bearer. Fall in."

"Into what?" the kid wanted to know.

"Into line," I said. "You walk ahead with me and do as I tell you. You're going to be courier and envoy and a lot of things. You're my official body-guard. You're my staff. Only don't break your other garter. Don't give the enemy any advantage."

So that was the way we fixed it. I marched ahead, with Pee-wee at my side holding the standard. He was a kind of a martial band, too, on account of his aluminum cooking set rattling and jingling in the phonograph horn. He looked very severe. I guess the women and children will never forget when he passed through poor, defenseless Bridgeboro. They're laughing yet. Talk about poor Belgium!

I marched along beside my official staff. I guess you know what I look like. You can see me on the cover of this book. That laugh is caused by Pee-wee. You can only see it, but oh, boy, you ought to hear it. Behind us came Westy and Dorry and Hunt Manners marching together, and behind them were Will Dawson and the Warner twins marching together. The expeditionary forces!

Behind us, after we got into town, all the kids followed along to see what it was all about, so pretty soon we had a crowd of about a couple of dozen all around us, yelling and hooting. And all the grown up people stopped and stared and then began to laugh. All the while Pee-wee looked straight ahead and his face was very severe.

We had two things to go by, the tree away off there on the ridge, and Pee-wee's compass. I carried that compass to help us in places where we couldn't see the tree. All we had to do was to go straight west.

The best way to hike a straight course with a compass is to get a very thin stick that's perfectly straight. A knitting needle is good only you must be sure not to use a steel one. You lay that across your compass. If you're going west you lay it across the east and west points. It's best to lay the compass down on something when you do that. Then you get a bead on the direction of the stick and pick out something that it points at. Then you hike straight for that thing. But there's no fun hiking a bee-line unless you're fair and square with yourself. If you go just a little bit out of your way to avoid something and try to make yourself think you're going straight, that's no fun. Because, one thing, you can't jolly a compass.

Now it was easy following that tree until we got down into town. Even then it was easy for a little distance on account of Central Avenue running east and west. We had good luck because our hike straight west down the hill took us right plunk into Central Avenue.

At the beginning of Central Avenue, where it kind of peters out at the foot of our hill, we stopped to make sure it went straight west. Because with a nice, long, straight street like that it's easy to fool yourself and say it goes straight west when it doesn't, quite. But Central Avenue did, because away down beyond the other end of it, and away across the river we could see that big tree up on the ridge. Central Avenue doesn't go all the way through town but we saw that as far as it did go it went straight west. We made good and sure. Because a bee-line hike is no good unless you're strict about it.

After we had gone a couple of blocks we couldn't see the tree any more on account of being right in the thick part of town. But we checked our course up with the compass on every corner and everybody crowded around laughing at us, and we had all the kids at our heels.

After we had gone about five blocks on Central Avenue we came to the place where it ends. It bunks right into another street that goes across it. Right across the street from the end of Central Avenue is a big house. There it was staring us right in the face. And right on the porch, plunk in front of the front door was a big fat man, staring us right in the face.

"Foiled!" I said.

"The bee-line goes right through the front door," Westy said. "That's just our luck. That's the kind of a house that has a hall going right through it. The bee-line goes right through that hall and in back is Monument Park."

"Right through the hall?" I said. "What good does that do us? It goes right through the man!"

"Now's the time for strategy," Pee-wee said.

I said, "Don't break your garter now, whatever you do, or all is lost."

"We've got to have a conference," he said.

CHAPTER VI
A PROPOSITION

I said, "Come on across the street and I'll consult with my official staff."

"That man looks invincible," Pee-wee said.

Westy said, "He looks immovable, that's sure."

I said, "I'm sorry now my official staff didn't bring a couple of British tanks with him."

That big, fat man just seemed to be saying, "They shall not pass."

Hunt Manners said, "Take a good look at him; does he look good-natured?"

We went across the street and stopped on the sidewalk of Grove Place right plunk in front of the big house. Then we all gathered around close to decide what we had better do next. There was quite a wide lawn in front of the house.

I said to my official staff, "Turn the standard around so the man can read it and notice if he smiles."

"He's too far away," Dorry said. "Why don't you send some one to reconnoiter and see if he smiles?"

"Send a spy," the kid whispered.

I said, "Don't tell your general what to do. You're appointed an envoy to go up to that porch and ask that man if it will be all right for Leader Blakeley of the Silver Fox Patrol B. S. A. to come up there and discuss whether we can cross his territory. Tell him if he wants to come down here and discuss it on neutral territory, you'll give him safe conduct. Do you know what that is? Take all your stuff with you and notice if he smiles. Go ahead and do just what I told you."

Honest, you'd have laughed if you could have seen that kid hiking up the walk across the lawn, rattling and jangling and hoisting his phonograph horn up on his shoulder. He tramped right up onto the porch and pretty soon I thought the man was kind of smiling.

Then, all of a sudden, good night, the kid raised his big megaphone up to his mouth to call through it and out fell the coffee-pot and the saucepan and his pair of sneakers and a lot of other stuff. I could see the big fat man just shaking.

"It's all right, come ahead!" the kid called through the megaphone.

When we came to the porch the man looked us over very funny, like. He didn't laugh, but I think he was having a hard job not to. Then I knew we'd win because I could see he was losing his morale.

He said, "Well, what's all this?"

I said, "This is the Silver Fox Patrol, First Bridgeboro Troop, Boy Scouts of America, and I'm their leader and we're on a bee-line hike and we can only go straight west."

He said, "And who are all those youngsters out on the sidewalk?"

I said, "They're just following us, they don't count."

He said, "Oh."

Then Pee-wee said, "I'll tell you about the scouts. When they start out to do a thing, they do it. See? Nothing can stop them. Maybe you know how a — a — cannon-ballgoes — —"

The man said, "I can imagine."

"You know what irresistible is?" the kid asked him. "Well, that's what we are."

The man said, "Oh, I see."

"Sure," Pee-wee said; "things that are hard, that's what we like."

"We eat 'em alive," Westy said.

I said to Pee-wee, "Do you know what insubordinate is? Well, that's what you are. Keep still while I talk. You're only my official staff."

The man said, "Well, you'd better pick up your official coffee-pot and saucepan, and state your terms. I'm not sure that I want an irresistible army of invasion going through my house."

"Irresistible armies of invasion aren't so bad," the kid piped up. "I'll tell you how it is — —"

"Keep still," I said, "or I'll put you in the megaphone." Then I said to the man, "We started from Blakeley's Hill and we pledged ourselves to go straight west— —"

"Without deviation," the kid shouted; "do you know what that means?"

I said, "We pledged ourselves to go straight west till we come to a certain tree on west ridge, and not to turn to the right or the left. So you see we'll have to go right through your house."

The man just sat there a little while, kind of thinking. I began to get anxious.

The kid said, "You know scouts always wipe their feet when they go in a house. Maybe they're kind of wild, but they always wipe their feet."

I could see the man was trying hard not to laugh, and he just sat there thinking. Then he said, "Since you admit scouts are wild I think I won't let them go through my house."

"Now, you see," I whispered to Pee-wee.

"Oh, they're not so very wild," he said.

All the time the man seemed to be thinking and he said, "If you could just climb over the house now; wouldn't that be better? Since you can do anything? I think you said you are irresistible."

Good night! I could have strangled that kid. I said, "We'd like to go the easiest way."

The man said, "Ah, then you don't really care for hard things? You are what might be called parlor scouts. I see. How about your appetites?"

"I'll tell you about our appetites!" the kid shouted.

I said, "Believe me, we can give you the best recommendations."

Then the man said, "Well, I'm sorry I can't let you go through the house."

I said, "You don't think we'd take any food, do you?"

He said, "Not that, but I'm afraid going through the house is out of the question. If you would care to try climbing over it I'll supply you with ladders. While my gardener is getting the ladders, cake and pie will be served. That is my proposition. If you care to take me up, all right. If not, we part friends. A man's house is his castle; I dare say you've heard that. If you are so wild and adventurous, show your mettle."

I said, "Didn't you see metal enough when my official staff spilled the saucepan and the coffee-pot and things?"

The man just said, "That is my offer. Cake, pie and the roof. Or nothing. You are the leader. What do you say?"

"Say yes," Pee-wee whispered to me.

Jiminies, that kid would climb over the Woolworth Building for a piece of pie.

CHAPTER VII
FAMINE

I said, "All right, we accept the offer."

"Just sit around and make yourselves at home," the man said. Then he went around the side of the house.

Jiminies, we didn't know what to make of that man. He was nice and sociable, and he seemed to be always trying not to laugh, and everybody knows that fat people are good-natured. And he seemed kind of to like us, too. Then why didn't he let us go through his house? That was what I wanted to know. If he had just been grouchy and ordered us off his place we wouldn't have been so surprised. But if he liked us well enough to go to some trouble on account of us, then why wouldn't he let us just go through his house?

I said, "We should worry. It won't be the first roof I climbed over. Only I don't understand it, that's all."

"It's a mystery," Pee-wee said. "Maybe he's got some kind of a plot. Hey?"

"Maybe he just wants to see if we can make good," Westy said.

Hunt said, "We'll give him a demonstration, all right."

"Maybe he meditates treachery," the kid said. I guess he got those words out of the movies.

"Well," I said, "we're here because we're here and we're going to stay here and see it through."

Pretty soon the plot grew thicker. We could hear that man talking over the telephone in the house. He was saying, "Yes, get here as soon as you can; a big haul."

"We're going to get hauled in," Pee-wee said. "He's calling up the police. What shall we do?" He looked frightened.

I said, "Stay right here; we're not quitters."

Then we could hear the man saying more. Gee williger, it had me guessing. He said, "Yes—yes. Oh, we could release them in a couple of months."

"Did you hear what he said?" Pee-wee whispered. "They'll release us in a couple of months. Come on, let's get out of here. What do you think it means?"

I said, "I don't know what it means. This man has me guessing. But we haven't done anything wrong. This is the Bee-line hike. Are we going to see it through or not?"

"We are!" they all said.

"All right," I said; "over the roof for us."

Dorry said, "I guess if Warde Hollister saw us now he'd say we're up against a real adventure."

"All he wants is to be a movie actor," Pee-wee said. "That's what he told me. He said scouts were just kids. I bet he'd have to admit that this is a dark mystery, all right."

Dorry said, "I know that man's name all right, it's Copley. Often I see him at the station."

"I knew he had something to do with cops," Hunt said. "I wonder how soon we'll know what's up his sleeve."

"I wonder how soon he'll pass the cake," Pee-wee said.

Anyway we didn't have to wait long for the refreshments. Mrs. Copley came out and passed around cake and cookies and things and she was nice and friendly. And while we were sprawling around on the porch eating, a man came around with a couple of ladders.

Mrs. Copley said, "I'll just lay this plate of cookies on the table and you boys can help yourselves while you're waiting for Mr. Copley to come out." Then she put the plate on a little wicker table over near the end of the porch. After that she went in the house.

Pee-wee said, "Those cookies are good, I'm going to have a couple more."

"Don't go over to the end of the porch," I told him. "We have to stay right here in front of the door; this is where the bee-line is."

"The bee-line can have a branch to it while we're waiting," the kid said. "Maybe the bee-line might be wider than you think—maybe."

"The bee-line runs just this side of those cookies," I said.

"You're a fine kind of a leader," he said, "to let her stand that plate over there. Is that what you call tactics?"

I said, "Why didn't you take a half dozen cookies when she passed them around the same as the rest of us did? You only took one."

"You don't call that tactics, do you?" Westy asked him.

"I've got some manners," the kid said.

I said, "Well, you haven't got any cookies. Look here." Then I showed him about a half a dozen. Oh, boy, they were nice and brown and crisp and they had nuts in them. The fellows all had about as many as a dozen cookies each, because Mrs. Copley had said, "Oh, do take more, I'm sure you're a hungry lot of scouts."

Pee-wee sat there on one of the steps watching us eat cookies. Every time he moved I said, "You stay right where you are. Remember, this is a bee-line hike."

Westy said, "These cookies are mighty good."

I said, "M—mmm, that's what they are."

Hunt said, "They're about the best I ever tasted. I've got eleven left."

"I bet they were just cooked," Dorry said.

I said, "Well, here goes another."

Will Dawson said, "That's one thing I like about the Raven Patrol; they have such good manners."

Pee-wee said, "Do you mean to tell me a bee-line can't have a — a — kind of a side track to it? Especially when we're sitting still?"

"Oh, positively not," I said. "A bee-line hasn't even got any waves or wrinkles in it. It's just as straight as a line drawn right through the middle of this cookie."

"Or this one," Westy said.

I said, "Yes, but this one is bigger. Do you see this cookie, Kid? Do you see that nut sticking up out of the end of it? Now suppose I draw a straight line — —"

"You make me tired!" the kid yelled, and he started to get up.

"My official staff will be seated," I said.

"You call this a kind of an army, don't you?" the kid shouted. "Do you mean to tell me that we can't make a flank movement?"

"Couldn't be did," I said; "remember your solemn pledge. Your duty is to stay as near to your beloved leader as you can. You just notice how these fellows obey me;now watch. Every scout will take a cookie in his right hand. When I say three they will start to eat. One, two, three. A scout is obedient — —"

"You mean a scout is resourceful," the kid shouted, jumping to his feet. All of a sudden he grabbed the coil of rope we had and, good night, if he didn't lasso the table and drag it over to him!

Just as he pulled the table within reach and was starting to fill his pockets with cookies, we heard some one call.

"Still! Just a minute! Don't move!"

CHAPTER VIII
REEL ADVENTURE

"All right. Good." I heard the voice say.

We all looked around and standing there on the lawn was Mr. Copley smiling and right beside him a fellow about twenty-five years old, I guess. He had an awful nice smile, with a regular good-natured, open face. Right beside him was a camera, and down on the ground was a big kind of a leather box with a handle to it. On that box was printed:
COPLEY FILM CORPORATION
THE WEEKLY ANIMATED NEWS
ALL THE WORLD IN PICTURES.
"G-o-o-d night!" I said. "We're pinched. We're in the movies!"
Mr. Copley said, "Boys, this is Mr. Tom Gilligan, of the Animated News. Our young friend of the megaphone is now famous. He will appear on the same film with President Harding leaving the White House in an automobile. Now we're going to give the people of the United States and Canada a glimpse of an amusing novelty, a scout bee-line hike. The next picture shows the young heroes climbing over a house which happens to be in their path."

So that's how it happened that part of our bee-line hike got on the screen. Most movie stars get a lot of money, but anyway we got a lot of cookies. And that's how it was that people away out in California could see our young hero lassoing a wild and woolly wicker table and massacring a whole tribe of cookies. We came right after President Harding. He was lucky because if we'd come along about ten seconds sooner on that film we'd have been climbing over the top of the White House. Just after us on that film came a railroad train that had been wrecked. That was one thing we escaped on our hike anyway.

Mr. Tom Gilligan was a nice fellow. He went around the country taking pictures of all sorts of things, famous men smiling and shaking hands, and houses burning down and people being crushed by falling buildings and everything. He said Pee-wee lassoing cookies was one of the best things he ever took. He said he'd like to take Pee-wee again.

I said, "Take him for all we care; you're welcome to him. Only don't bring him back."

It wasn't hard climbing over that house, but Tom Gilligan made us do a lot of fancy things. He said people would like that. So we had Pee-wee roll down the shed in back of the house and spill all the stuff out of his megaphone. It's worth thirty cents and the war tax to see that. You'll see me standing up on the peak of the house hugging the chimney, and holding my hand above my eyes and scanning the distant country to the West. This is what it said on that picture: "Scout Blakeley picking out the bee-line to the West, guided by his distant beacon."

It was easy sliding down the roof in back; we just slid down onto the back porch and down to the ground.

In back of that house is Monument Park. It isn't very big, you can put it in your pocket. Tom Gilligan said he'd go a little farther with us to see what we ran into next.

Now from Monument Park we could see the big poplar tree good and plain. The reason for that was partly on account of the park being so open and partly on account of the land beyond being low, because all the while we were going down toward the river. West of the park there aren't so many houses because in Bridgeboro a lot of people don't like to live too near the river. Some people are crazy. The houses down that way are not so big and they're not so close together.

The only thing that stood in our way in the park was the big wooden fence, sort of, with all the soldiers' names on it. It wasn't so very long and we might have gone around it only I decided that our path was right about through the middle of it. So we crawled under it.

Then right ahead of us was River Road, crossing our path. We stopped and took a squint and used our compass and decided that our path was between two houses.

Tom Gilligan said, "I think it's right through that house on the left."

I said, "No, sir, it's right across the lawn between the two houses. You just want us to get into some trouble so you can show the whole of the United States and Canada. I know you."

He said, "You kids take another look at that tree. Your bee-line is just— exactly—precisely—across the side porch of that house with the brown shingles. Now you see."

I said, "You're right. I've got to send my official staff to that house for permission to cross neutral territory."

But when I looked around for my official staff, there he was standing stark still about ten yards behind us.

I said, "Come ahead, official staff. What's the matter with you?"

He said, "Do you know whose house that is? I didn't know because I never came toward it this way before. It's Warde Hollister's house. I can tell by the bay window."

"That suits me," I said.

"You'll—you'll have to use diplomacy," Pee-wee said. "I know that fellow."

"Believe me," I said, "I've got the diploma for diplomacy. You fellows camp right here and leave that fellow to me. Here's where we not only cross neutral porches, but here's where we take a prisoner, too. In about ten minutes I'll have the enemy eating out of my hand."

"What?" Pee-wee just blurted out.

"Eating out of my hand," I said. "You know what eating means, don't you?"

"S——sure I do," the kid said.

CHAPTER IX
DIPLOMACY

I left the fellows where they were and went across the street, keeping straight west. Away over on the ridge, beyond the river and beyond Little Valley, I could see the big tree good and clear against the sky. It seemed sort of lonely up there. I said to myself, "You wait, old tree, we're coming straight along." Gee whiz, I was kind of glad that our destination was a tree and not some building or other. You'll never catch me planting the Silver Fox emblem on the roof of an apartment house. I'm not saying anything against buildings, but one thing, I have no use for them. My mother says it's good to have a roof over your head, but I'd rather have it underneath me because you can have more fun climbing over it, that's what I told her. That's why I believe in roofs. But I like trees better. I like trees better than anything except holidays. The thing I like worst of all is algebra.

I went straight over to that house and stopped on the sidewalk right plunk in front of the part of the porch that sticks out past the end of the house. Then I gave the Silver Fox call good and loud. As soon as Pee-wee heard me he started shouting it through the megaphone. It sounded like a Silver Fox with a cold.

Pretty soon the door opened, and—good night, there was Warde Hollister.

I said, "Tag, you're It. Will you please come down here on neutral territory? We belong to the League of Notions and we can't cross any frontiers—I mean front yards."

He said, "What do you want here?"

I said, "Answered in the affirmative. We're here because we're here and the end of your front porch is in the way. It sticks out like the West Front just before the armistice."

"You must be crazy," he said.

"Positively guaranteed," I told him. "We're so crazy that a crazy quilt is sensible compared to us."

"If you want to see me, come up here," he said. "Are you afraid to come up?"

"Afraid?" I said. "Didn't we go right into the same film with President Harding? Who's afraid of you? Not I, quoth he. I can't come up because I can't go off the track and your front steps are about thirty feet too far north."

"You're one of those scouts," he said.

"Tell me something new," I said; "did you think I didn't know that? Maybe you don't know I'm a famous movie star; we're all stars, we're known as the big dipper. Did you ever hear of Douglas Saving Banks?"

"Sure," he said.

"Well, I'm not him," I told him. "Come on down, will you?"

He looked across the street and saw the rest of the fellows and I guess he must have seen the big leather box with Copley Film Corporation on it. Anyway, he just stared. Then he came over to the end of the porch and sat on the railing and said,

"What do you want, anyway? One of you fellows was here yesterday. I told him I didn't want to bother with you."

"That was my official staff," I said. "We don't bother with him either; we carry him as excess baggage. That's the Japanese junk man. Did you ever hear that song? It's dedicated to him. We should worry about the scouts. But you see this is the way it is. We've got the movie people after us and we can't get rid of them. They're trying to stir up a new war here in Bridgeboro after everything is all peaceful again and school is closed. We're on a bee-line hike to a big tree over on west ridge, and we have to go straight no matter what's in the way. Gee whiz, it's not much fun.

"But, anyway, that big fellow thinks if we try to climb across your porch it will be a good idea for you to come out and look very grouchy and try to stop us; maybe you could look that way if you tried to, hey? And then we'll be very sweet and nice and give you a big hunk of candy and you'll say the boy scouts are all right and you'd like to join them. Of course you don't have to really join them. All you have to do is be in the animated news, all the world in pictures, right in the same film with President Harding. Maybe you wouldn't care to be a movie actor, hey? You should worry, it will soon be over. Mr. Gilligan, he just wants to show how fellows get to be scouts. It's propaganda. After it's all over you can go in the house again, and we'll beat it for the river. You don't have to really join, it's only in the picture. See? It won't be a real chunk of candy we hand you so as to show that we're kind and generous. It will be a rock. But it will look like candy. It will be rockcandy."

CHAPTER X
THE BEE-LINE

So if you saw that animated-news-of-all-the-world film and saw Pee-wee Harris handing a nice piece of candy to a boy who isn't a scout, you'll know it wasn't real candy he was handing him. That's why he had such a generous, kind look on his face. A scout is brotherly—especially with rocks.

That was the only movie play I ever wrote. I didn't write that, but I thought it up. Tom Gilligan said it was fine. One good thing, there were only three pictures in it. It was a scout propaganda picture. It was called Kindness Wins, or Letting Him Have a Rock. Only Tom Gilligan cut out the last part of the name.

That picture showed us all climbing over the railing of that porch, and then it showed Warde Hollister coming out and shaking his fist at us. He did that fine for a fellow that wasn't a scout. Then it showed us telling him about our adventures and showing him the coffee-pot and all the cooking things. And then it showed our generous little hero handing him a nice piece of candy. After that the fellow said he'd like to join the scouts because they had such a lot of fun. And so he joined and they all lived happily forever and forever.

After Tom Gilligan had taken the pictures just the way he wanted them Warde Hollister threw the piece of rock at a tree and missed it because he wasn't a scout—because scouts always aim straight, only they don't throw rocks, but if they did they wouldn't miss.

"Now you're in the movies," I said, "and you're satisfied because that's just what you wanted. And we thank you a lot."

He said, "Where are you going now?"

"Oh, just across the porch if you'll let us," I told him, "and then across the river in a bee-line. Some job, hey? Then straight for that big tree on the ridge. You look up there late this evening and see if there's a fire burning.

Then you'll know we're roasting potatoes. Do you know what I think? I think the bee-line takes us right through the haunted house across the river. I bet you're glad you're only a scout in the movies. Pity the poor scouts, hey?"

He said, kind of hesitating, "I'm not afraid of haunted houses."

"Are you afraid of snakes?" Pee-wee piped up.

He said, "No, I'm not. I—like roasted potatoes, though."

"How many do you like?" the kid asked him.

"As many as I can get," Warde said. "And I'd like to go with you fellows if you'll let me."

Westy said, "Do you mean you'd like to join the scouts?"

He said, "Yes, I do."

Tom Gilligan was standing there with his camera over his shoulder and his big leather bag in his hand, all ready to go away. I guess he was going back to the station and I was sorry because I liked that fellow.

He said to Warde, "You're a wise young fellow, you are. Go in for the real thing and don't bother with imitations. What's the use of jumping off a cliff made of pasteboard when you've got real roofs to climb over? What's the use of doing stunts in a studio when you can go on a bee-line hike across the country? You're a wise young fellow, you are. You stick to the boy scouts; they'll keep you moving."

Then he said, "Well, so long, kids." And away he went.

I said, "Come over here right close to us and keep near us, Warde. We're keeping this bee-line as narrow as we can."

He jumped up on the porch rail right beside us. The others were all right there, squatting on the porch or sitting on the rail. We could see across the river and past the old ramshackle buildings there and right over the village of Little Valley to the ridge. That big tree stood up higher than all the others and it seemed just as if it were all alone off there. I guess it was about one o'clock then.

I said, "We're going to cook some eats as soon as we get to the river, because we like to eat near where there's water. Then we'll have to think how we'll get across."

"Did you come straight all the way from your house?" Warde wanted to know.

"Just as straight as we could," I said. "If we side-stepped anything we didn't mean to. There's no use saying you're going to do a thing, and then kid yourself about it and not do it. Maybe a bee-line hike is kind of crazy, but it's hard, too. It's easy to make yourself think the line runs between two houses when it doesn't. It's sort of the same when you get to be a scout. It's like a bee-line hike—sort of."

We all just sat there and nobody said anything until Westy said, "That's right."

"Maybe you don't understand," Dorry said.

Warde said, "Yes, I do understand."

After that nobody said anything, not even Pee-wee, and we just sat there.

"Sure you can go with us," I told him. "And just as I said, you'll see we're kind of crazy. But just the same we don't sneak around and we don't turn back; not till we have to, anyway. You can join the scouts just for the fun of it if you want; the same as you can start on a bee-line hike and go zigzagging around the easiest way if you want to. Maybe you don't understand just exactly what I mean," I said to him. "Anyway there's a place to be filled in my patrol."

"Could I get in—maybe?" he asked.

I said, "Sure you could. Who's stopping you? Even one of our fellows came after you, didn't he? And you see for yourself how the movie people come after us. You don't see us running after them. They know where adventures are, all right."

"And no war tax either," Westy said.

"And plenty of eats," Pee-wee piped up.

Then for a little while again none of us said anything.

CHAPTER XI
EATS

So that's how Warde Hollister got to be a Silver-plated Fox. Already he has four merit badges and he's crazy like the rest of us, only more so. If he keeps on, maybe he'll be as crazy as I am because I wasn't so crazy when I started.

And that shows how you never can tell what you may run into on a bee-line hike. But when it comes to running into things just you wait till you get to the next chapter.

Now from Warde Hollister's house we went straight for the river. There aren't many houses down there and the land is low and we could see the tree all the time. We had to climb over a couple of fences and over the storage shed of the boat club, and we had to crawl under Benton's ice house that stands on piles.

Then we came to the river. There are willow trees down there and we sat under one of them to eat our lunch. We started a fire and I made some flapjacks. Warde Hollister said that was the first time he had ever eaten lunch out in the open like that and he said it was fine.

I said, "Have all you want, don't be bashful. They're nice and tender, they're intended for tenderfeet."

He said, "Is that what I am?"

"You're not anything yet," I told him; "you have to pass some tests; endurance tests and things like that. I'm going to introduce you to our scoutmaster and he'll take care of you."

"Eating flapjacks is an endurance test," Pee-wee said.

Westy said, "Sure, if you can eat these you can do anything."

"Are some of those things hard?" Warde asked me. "I mean those tests," he said.

"They're not so hard as these flapjacks," Hunt Manners told him.

"Oh, is that so?" I said. "I notice hard things don't trouble you much."

He said, "The pleasure is mine; flop me another one, will you?"

"They call these things stove-lids up at Temple Camp," Will Dawson told Warde.

I said, "Yes, and you're a pretty good stove-lifter, all right."

"I bet you have a lot of fun, you fellows," Warde said, kind of laughing.

"Sure," I told him, "we have so much fun that even the weeping willows die crying from laughing so hard. If you had this patrol to look after your hair would soon turn white. My teeth are white already from worrying. We remind ourselves of balloons instead of foxes. We should worry. You're in for it now and you can't help yourself. The worst is yet to come. Don't you care, smile and look pleasant. You might have done worse, you might have got into the Raven Patrol."

"What's the matter with the Raven Patrol?" the kid shouted, trying to eat a flapjack and shout at the same time.

"One good thing about them," Westy said.

"What's that?" Hunt asked him.

"That's that they're not here," Westy said.

"The Raven Patrol will be — it'll be flourishing when the Silver Foxes are all busted up!" the kid shouted.

"Sure," I told him, "but not until then. Wait till you see that bunch," I said to Warde. "They're dead and they don't know it."

"They died laughing at P. Harris," Westy said.

"You think you're so smart, don't you?" the kid shouted. "One of our patrol is camp librarian at Temple Camp."

"They're all highbrows," Westy said. "They think Scott's Emulsion is by Sir Walter Scott. They're all busy studying monotony in that patrol."

"Do you mean to tell me that—that—that Ravens——" the kid began yelling.

"You see how ravens can go up in the air," I said to Warde. "Now you know why they're called the Raving Ravens. They're all right as long as you don't feed them meat. They think you can do good turns riding on a merry-go-round."

"What's the second-hand scout?" Warde wanted to know.

"Good night," I said, "don't make me laugh. You mean a second-class scout. Of course there are slightly used scouts, 1915 models, but you wouldn't call them exactly second-hand. First comes the tenderfoot, then the second-class scout and then the first-class scout—and above that are the Silver Foxes in a class by themselves."

"That's because they can't get anybody to go in the class with them," Pee-wee shouted.

Westy said, "Well, here we are talking about classes in vacation time. In a minute we'll be talking about arithmetic. Let's talk of something pleasant while we're eating."

I said, "Sure, let's talk of something pleasant. I didn't start talking about the Ravens. The question is how are we going to follow a bee-line across the river? I wish the equator went across the river and we could walk on that."

CHAPTER XII
BLACK OR WHITE

We knew it would be pretty easy going after we got across the river. But getting across the river, that was the question. We knew well enough that we couldn't swim straight across on account of the tide running out. It would have carried us downstream. The river isn't very wide there and it isn't much of a swim across, only if we tried it we'd land east of our course.

Westy said, "We're up against it now. What are we going to do?"

"If we wait till the tide is full," Hunt said, "we'll have to sit around here till about eleven o'clock to-night."

I said, "Do you suppose the rope would reach across?"

"Sure it would," Dorry answered, "only how are we going to get it across?"

"Throw it," Pee-wee said.

"And what will hold it there?" I asked him. "Besides, what good is the rope as long as we haven't got our bathing suits? You don't expect us to walk on the rope, do you?"

"Oh, here comes a boat!" Dorry shouted. "See it? It's just coming around the bend. There are two men in it."

"Are they nice men?" I asked him.

"What are you talking about?" Pee-wee shouted. "They're a quarter of a mile away!"

I said, "That wouldn't prevent them from being nice men. Your uncle is all the way over in Europe and he's a nice man."

"All I can see is their backs," Westy said.

I said, "Well, as far as I can tell from their backs they look as if they might be nice men. Maybe we can get them to carry the end of the rope across and fasten it on the other side."

"Yes, and what will we do then?" the kid wanted to know.

"Then we'll say 'thank you,'" I told him.

"Yes, and what then?"

I said, "Why, then we'll ask them to row us across keeping the boat close to the rope. They could never row straight across with the tide running this way."

"I don't see why the tide has to be running out just now," Hunt said.

"Neither do I," I said; "especially as it's just going to turn around and come right in again. It might as well stay in. It goes to a lot of trouble for nothing. We should worry."

Pretty soon the boat was nearly opposite us, and I shouted, "Hey, Mister, will you give us a lift across?"

Pee-wee whispered to me, "I know who that front man is; he's a detective. You better look out how you speak to him. That's Detective Pinchem."

As soon as the kid spoke I saw that he was right. I shouted, "Hey, Mister Pinchem, will you give us a lift across? We're lost, strayed or stranded."

The men in the boat started for the shore and Mr. Pinchem called, "Hello, you scouts, what are you doing here?"

I said, "We've got as much right here as this river has. It's in our way and we want to get across."

Pee-wee whispered to me very anxious-like, "You better look out how you talk to him, he's a detective. He can arrest us if he wants to."

Westy said, "Why should we be afraid? We haven't taken anything."

I said, "I'm not so sure about that. We're taking a hike. Maybe if we can't prove it belongs to us — — "

"You're crazy," the kid said.

"I know a fellow who got arrested for stealing third base when he was on the High School team," Hunt said.

I said, "Hey, Mr. Pinchem, can we get arrested for taking a hike that doesn't belong to us?"

He just laughed because he knows we're all crazy. He said, "Well, what's on your mind now? You want to be arrested, huh?"

"We didn't say that," the kid spoke up.

Mr. Pinchem just stepped out of the boat and gave him a shove and said, "You've been stealing somebody's phonograph, huh? I'll have to look into that."

I said, "Good night, go ahead and look into it. All you'll see is a lot of junk."

Mr. Pinchem and that other man just stood there laughing and he said, "Well, what's on your minds? You want to get across, do you?"

I said, "We want to get across in a bee-line. Do you see that tree just across the river? The one near the shore. That's in a bee-line with that big tree away up there on west ridge. So if you'd be willing to take the end of this rope across and fasten it to that tree, then maybe you can row us over without drifting with the tide. We have to go in a bee-line."

He said, "Oh, that's it, is it? Well, now, suppose that bee-line takes you right through the County Jail. What then?"

Pee-wee looked kind of frightened.

"That's up to the County Jail," I said. "If the County Jail doesn't get out of the way, we go through it. Didn't you ever hear that boy scouts are invincible?"

Pee-wee said, "They're not—exactly—they're not always so very invincible. See? They have to be courteous. If you asked us not to go through the jail, we wouldn't. See?"

Westy said, "We've even been through public school, we're so smart."

44

Mr. Pinchem said, "I'd say you've been through an ice house, you're so fresh. Well, I'll see what we can do for you. I hope you'll always keep as straight as you're going now."

I said, "We always go straight; we don't go around much. We're always wide awake except when we're asleep."

He said, "Well, you're so wide awake, you didn't happen to see anything of a man around here? A man with a cap and a brown sweater?"

"He may be a colored man," the other man said.

"What color?" Pee-wee said, all excited.

"Why, black, maybe," Mr. Pinchem said; "or maybe not. A pretty rough looking customer. Didn't happen to notice any one around here, huh?"

"Is he a murderer?" Pee-wee asked.

"Well, I guess he'd be willing to be," Mr. Pinchem said. "He stole a skiff from the boat club in Northvale and it was found empty down below here in the marshes."

"Do you want me to help you find him?" the kid piped up.

Mr. Pinchem's friend said, "He held up an auto on the state road above Northvale last night. He fired two shots; got away with some jewelry and about seven hundred dollars. The chauffeur thought he was black but he wasn't sure; didn't see his face."

"He—eh—I hope you catch him," our young hero said.

He didn't seem to be quite as anxious to do the catching as he had been about a minute before.

CHAPTER XIII
BANDITS AND THINGS

I said, "Grab hold of this rope, Detective Harris, if you want to get across the river."

So that's the way we got across, going straight west, even while the tide was running out good and strong. Mr. Pinchem rowed over with one end of the rope, and the tide carried him about fifty yards downstream before he made the other shore. Then he got out and dragged the boat back upstream and tied the rope to the tree just where we told him to.

We had to make two trips across, but it was easy keeping our course because all we had to do was to keep hold of the rope and work the boat along with our hands.

I guess those men didn't think we could be much help to them; anyway they didn't hire Pee-wee to foil the bandit the way men do in stories. I'd like to see that kid capturing a bandit. Judging by the way he treats ice cream cones there wouldn't be much left of the bandit. I'm not crazy about bandits, anyway, but some fellows are. Anyway, I'd like a blue one better than a black one because that's my patrol color.

But, anyway, this is the way those men thought it was. Northvale is about three or four miles above Bridgeboro. It's right on the river and there's a boat club up there. So when they found that boat in the marshes down near Bridgeboro I guess they thought that fellow had left the boat and maybe was hiding somewhere around there. Because, anyway, it would be pretty hard for him to get through the marshes to the railroad track, that's sure.

Now after those men left us they started rowing back up the river and they didn't get along very fast on account of the tide being against them. Gee whiz, I'd kind of like to be a detective if I was a man, but I wouldn't want to be a truant officer.

So now our bee-line hike was about half over and we had traveled in a pretty straight line. I'm not saying that we didn't go even a yard to the right or left, because, gee, that would be impossible, but I bet we went in a pretty straight line. We didn't vary our course any just to save trouble, that's sure.

Now from the river there is open country till you get to Little Valley. The only thing that stands in the way is Riverview Park. That used to be an amusement park. They closed it up during the war because they needed the horses on the merry-go-round for ambulances in France; that's what Harry Donnelle said. He lives in Little Valley.

Anyway, they never opened that park again. Gee whiz, I didn't care much because we're always up at Temple Camp in the summer. All you could do there was spend money. You can have more fun for nothing.

So the only trouble we would have between the river and Little Valley was the board fence around that old park, and you don't call a board fence an obstacle, I hope.

Our young hero couldn't get that bandit out of his mind. He said, "I bet he's a pretty desperate robber, hey? To fire two shots."

"Sure," Westy said, "if he had only fired one it wouldn't have been so bad. And to get away with seven hundred dollars, too."

"If it had been only three or four hundred dollars I wouldn't say anything," I said. "But seven hundred is too much."

"It's grand larceny," the kid said.

"I don't call it so very grand," I told him. "If you think it's grand to steal seven hundred dollars, you've got some funny ideas. I suppose if a man stole about ten thousand dollars you'd call that magnificent larceny."

"You're crazy," Pee-wee shouted. "Grand larceny is a kind of a crime."

I said, "Well, I'm a scout, and I don't call larceny grand."

"It's a crime," Pee-wee shouted, "and he can get a long sentence for it."

"He ought to get a whole paragraph for a crime like that," I told him.

"Do you think maybe we'll run into him?" the kid wanted to know.

"Not if we see him first," I said. "I guess a man who is guilty of wayhigh robbery wouldn't hang around here."

"Sometimes scouts catch fugitives," Pee-wee said.

"More often they catch the dickens," Hunt said. "Come on, forget it."

"Sure," I said; "keep in a bee-line and you'll always go straight."

CHAPTER XIV
THE HAUNTED WHEEL

I guess maybe it's a half a mile across that old amusement park. All the land there is low; we could see right over the top of Little Valley as you might say, and the big tree away off there on the ridge stood out good and plain. Maybe that was partly because the sun was getting over that way. Anyway, I know that about a couple of hours later the tree looked as if it were all kind of spangled with gold like a Christmas tree. It seemed sort of as if the sun was going ahead to get the tree all decorated for us.

Westy said, "The sun's beginning to get over to the west. See?"

I said, "It's going to beat us to the tree, too."

So you can see from what I told you that it was easy to follow a straight course right through that old park. Sometimes we had to clamber over piles of old boards and we had to work our way kind of in and out through the old rotten trestle of the scenic railway. That thing crossed our path like a big, long, wriggling snake. Some of the old booths were boarded up and some of them were all falling to pieces. The concrete basin that used to be a swimming pool was all full of rubbish. And the little platform away way up, that the man used to do the dive of death from, was all falling to pieces. Some places we had to climb over the old ramshackle booths, but that was easy.

All of a sudden Westy stopped short and said, "Look ahead; do you know what?"

"What?" I asked him.

"See that old ferris-wheel?" he said. "We're going to run plunk right into it."

I took a good squint and sure enough it was right in a bee-line with our beacon. It wasn't across our path but it was lengthways with our path. It was so narrow that we might have gone past on either side of it, but just the same it was right plunk in our path. It was quite a long ways ahead.

Once, when Westy and I were going through that old park on our way home from Little Valley we got a good scare on account of that old ferris-wheel. And that's what started people thinking it was haunted. Maybe you've heard of haunted houses but I bet you never heard of a haunted ferris-wheel.

That time we went through there—oh, I guess it was a couple of years ago. Anyway, it was in the night and everything was as dark as licorice bars. Maybe you never ate those, but they're mighty good, they're black. All of a sudden we heard a kind of a creaking noise and we couldn't make out where it was. Sometimes it sounded just as if it might be a person.

We followed that noise the best we could and pretty soon we came to the old wheel. It isn't so big, that wheel. And it isn't so little either. Then we could hear the sound good and plain and it was up in the wheel. It sounded pretty spooky. Sometimes it was a noise like some one crying. And then it would kind of die away.

When we got home we told about it and Mr. Ellsworth (he's our scoutmaster) said it was probably just the wind blowing in that creaky old thing. But after that, all the kids in Bridgeboro said the wheel was haunted. If you say a place is haunted, it's haunted.

But one thing, it kept the kids away from the old park. Because, anyway, they weren't supposed to go there. Gee whiz, I can't say whether I'm afraid of a ghost or not because I never saw one, but I know that white is their patrol color. Anyway, if I were a ghost I wouldn't hang out in a ferris-wheel, I know that. I guess they're half crazy, anyway, because there used to be one in the old tumbled-down schoolhouse in North Bridgeboro. Jiminy, I should think he could have found a better place than that to stay in. But my father says it's pretty hard to find places to live in these days. We should worry, the woods for us.

CHAPTER XV
A SCOUT IS OBSERVANT

Westy said, "I wonder how our old friend the ghost is?"

I said, "If we meet him we'll take him along with us. He ought to be good on a bee-line hike because he can go right through anything."

I said, "If it wasn't for Warde Hollister I'd take him into my patrol. I've got every kind of a freak in there now except a ghost."

"You haven't got me," Pee-wee shouted.

I said, "No, that's one kind of a freak I haven't got."

"If you could have a ghost and a bandit in this patrol we'd be complete," Westy said.

"I'm bad enough," Warde Hollister said.

I said, "Sure, we're satisfied if you are. Take us for better or worse; you'll probably find us a good deal worse."

Warde said, "It's been good fun so far."

"You haven't seen anything yet," I told him. "Wait till you get up to Temple Camp. Even the laughing brook is all the time giggling at us. Wait till you see the raving Ravens."

"That's all right," Pee-wee piped up. "Up there people in the village always smile at us — grown-up people."

"It's a wonder they don't laugh out loud," I said.

All of a sudden, as we were going along, Pee-wee grabbed me by the shoulder and whispered, "Look!"

"Have a heart," I told him; "don't knock me down. What is it?"

"Look!" he whispered. "Look! Where that board is broken."

Then I knew what he meant. About twenty feet off our path was a kind of an old tumbled-down shack. It was boarded up in front with old odds and ends of boards that were not painted. There was quite a big piece gone from one of the boards, and as I looked through that I could see a face.

"Shh, do you see it?" I whispered to Westy. Then I kind of urged the fellows along the path because I didn't want us to be standing right there in front of that hole.

"What—what did I tell you?" Pee-wee whispered, all excited.

"You didn't tell me anything," I said. "Shh, don't talk so loud. Come on, let's walk along a little further. Do you want him to see us?"

"Did you see?" Pee-wee whispered, so excited he could hardly speak. "It was a black man. It's the bandit. I discovered him."

"What are we going to do about it?" I asked the other fellows. "There's somebody in there."

"Sure there is," two or three of them said.

Will Dawson said, "I saw him plain; he was standing in back of a box. He was a colored man, all right."

"I was the first to discover him," Pee-wee whispered.

I said, "All right, findings is keepings; you can have him, he's yours. Now are you satisfied?"

By that time we were about ten yards past the shack, standing all in a group. The person inside couldn't see us through the opening in front of the shack but for all we knew he might be peeking at us through some little crack or hole. It made me feel funny to think that he was in there staring at us and we not able to see him.

I said, "Come on, let's walk along just as if we didn't suspect anything; we can talk while we're walking."

So we started along and Dorry said, "The best thing is for one of us to run ahead to Little Valley and tell the police there."

"You'll find the police department standing in front of the post office," I said. "That's where he usually hangs out."

I guess the only one of us that hadn't spoken at all was Warde Hollister. All of a sudden he said, "What's the good of notifying the police? Scouts aren't afraid, are they? Harris is the one who discovered him. So he ought to be the one to go back and capture him."

"That shows how much you know about scouts," Pee-wee said. "Scouts are supposed to be cautious. If you're reckless, then you're not a good scout. See? Maybe I'd like to go back and capture that bandit, but I have to make a sacrifice and not do it. See?"

I said, "Sure, it's as clear as mud. Let's sit down here just as if we were going to take a rest; let's sprawl on the ground just as if we weren't thinking about that shack at all. Then we can talk about what we'd better do."

"Maybe the ground is better a little further along," the kid said.

"This is all right," Westy said.

So we sat down right in our path and Will Dawson and Dorry Benton started playing mumbly-peg, so that if the man in the shack saw us he wouldn't be suspicious. Because if he thought we had seen him and were going to tell, he'd probably start running away.

"Don't look back," Westy said. "What are we going to do? We can't capture him ourselves, can we?"

"The only way would be to sprinkle a little salt on him," Warde Hollister said.

It seemed sort of funny the way that fellow talked because all of us had seen that black face in the shack and a bandit is no joke, especially a negro bandit, but any color is bad enough. Anyway, I was glad to see that Warde was getting crazy like the rest of us. But I didn't know till another minute how crazy he really was.

53

CHAPTER XVI

SUSPENSE

I said, "All right, but it's pretty serious. There's that black man in there. If we start toward Little Valley or back toward Bridgeboro he'll be suspicious and escape. We know where he is and maybe he doesn't know we know. How are we going to notify Mr. Pinchem or anybody else, that's the question?"

Westy said, "Maybe one of us could sneak away and hurry to Little Valley."

"Yes, and maybe he'll sneak away too," I said.

"Maybe we could start a fire and send up a smudge signal," said Dorry.

"Sure, and make it good and black because he's a negro," Warde said.

I said, "It's all very well to joke, but we have that man as good as caught. What are we going to do about it?"

"Some one hustle to Little Valley," Westy said.

"A smudge signal," said Dorry and Will.

Warde Hollister said, "Well, of course I don't know so much about scouts because I'm not really a member yet."

"They're supposed to be observant," the kid said.

"And brave," Warde said.

"Sure, but they have to be cautious," the kid said.

"They're supposed to use sense," I put in.

Warde said, "Well, I'm not afraid of what's in there. Maybe I'm not so observant, but that fellow in there can't scare me. If Pee-wee doesn't want to go and nab him, I'll go and nab him myself."

Just then he got up and started for the shack.

"Come back!" I said. "You're crazy!"

Pee-wee grabbed him by his jacket and said, all excited, "Do you want to get killed? Do you want to get killed? Sit down! Do you want to get killed? Don't you know that man fired two shots?"

Westy said, "Come back, you fool!"

Hunt jumped up and grabbed him and he and Pee-wee both tried to hold him back. "Sit down, sit down!" they said. "Do you want to get shot?"

Warde just shook them off, and he said, "This kid came up to my house yesterday and gave me a lot of stuff about scouts being courageous and brave and intrepid — — "

"Let me tell you what intrepid means," the kid said, half crazy. "It — it — it — has — it has two meanings — kind of."

"A scout is supposed to risk his life and get the Gold Cross," Warde said. "That's just what you told me."

Gee whiz, before we realized it he was half way over to the shack.

"We'd better run," the kid said.

"Stay where you are," Westy told him.

I said, "That fellow has been reading crazy adventure stories, about kids capturing highwaymen and all that."

"That's what he gets from lying in the hammock and reading Deadeye Dick," Will said.

"What — what shall we do?" the kid asked.

By that time Warde Hollister was right close up to the shack. Gee whiz, I had to admit he was reckless. He just walked right up and caught hold of that loose board and gave it a yank. We just waited, cold. Every second we were expecting to hear a shot and then see that big ugly black man come dashing out.

"No wonder," Westy said; "his brain is full of boy scouts who murder and all that — that isn't — listen!"

It was just the sound of Warde pulling down that old rotten board and crawling through. We were all in such suspense that we could hardly speak. The kid was nearly dead with fright.

"Listen—shh!" Westy said.

"It's a scuffle," I said.

Then, all of a sudden, oh, boy, I can hear it now, there was a loud, sudden report like a pistol shot.

We just stood there trembling. None of us moved or spoke.

CHAPTER XVII

THE HERO

When Will Dawson spoke his voice was hoarse. "Let's go—we've got to go and look in," he said.

Westy just gulped. He said, "Wait a second—listen."

"It's awful," Ralph Warner said. "We—we can't just stand here. What shall we do?"

Pee-wee was as white as snow. He just stood there gulping.

"We'll—we'll have—to—tell his—his mother," one of the fellows said.

Just then, good night, you'll hardly believe it when I tell you. Out came one of those old boards just as if some one was kicking it, and there was Warde Hollister dragging out the poor limp black man by the neck. The man's arms were flopping about this way and that and Warde threw him down flat on the ground. Then he made his hands into two cups and slapped them together.

"Just one more shot to finish him," he said. It sounded just exactly like a pistol.

"There he is," Warde said; "and he'll never frighten good little boy scouts again. Nobody will ever get another prize for hitting him in the eye with a baseball. His glorious career as a target is over. Step up, lads, and take a look at him."

Oh, boy, I guess we never felt so silly in our lives. Poor bandit, he was just one of those figures that sit in a chair and are pelted with baseballs, three shots for a dime. "Every time you hit the nigger!" That's what the man used to call. When some one hit him a good hard crack he'd topple off the seat and then the man would give you a kewpie doll or maybe an ash-tray. The poor old wooden "nigger" had been packed away and all we had seen was his black face sticking up above some old boxes.

I said to Warde, laughing good and hard, "You knew it all the time, didn't you?"

He just said, "A scout is observant. Do I get the Gold Cross?"

Westy said, "I don't think you get the Gold Cross, but we ought to get leather medals, I know that. We're a fine outfit of scouts not to know an old 'hit-the-nigger' target from a bandit."

Warde just kicked the poor old black man. I guess the black man didn't care, because he was used to being pelted in the face. I wouldn't want that job.

Then Warde said, "Scout Harris is to blame for this horrible murder. Did you ever hear of mental suggestion?" Gee, that fellow's smart.

"Is that what you killed him with?" I said.

He said, "If you're hunting for a thing, everything looks like that thing. Harris had bandits on his brain, so one look at this thing was enough for you fellows."

"If you're looking for—for—a piece of pie," Pee-wee piped up, "will everything be pie?"

"Posilutely," I said. "Just the same as when you're in Hamburg everything looks like ham. It's the same only different. Just the same as all the buildings in Paris are made of plaster of paris. Just the same as the raving Ravens are afraid of wooden dummies. What's the answer?"

"Answer to what?" he shouted.

"Anything," I said. "It depends on what the question is. Warde Hollister is a better scout than any of us. Deny it if you dare, quoth I. He has performed the most heroic act since Artie Van Arlen, patrol leader of the Ravens, killed a couple of hours waiting for a train for Temple Camp. They don't care what they kill, those scouts."

We put the baseball target back where he belonged and I guess he's dead yet for all I know. He faced a good many bee-lines, that's one sure thing. Anyway, we should bother about him because we had our own bee-line hike to finish, only the worst was yet to come.

CHAPTER XVIII
ONE, TWO, THREE, GO!

After that, for as much as about ten yards, we didn't have any more adventures. Then we had to climb over the band-stand, but that wasn't much of an adventure.

The next thing we passed was a lot of cookies I had in my pocket. I passed them around. After that we came to the place where Daredevil Dennell used to go up in a balloon and just beyond there is the ferris-wheel.

Now it was about half past three or so, or maybe four o'clock, when we came near the ferris-wheel. The sun was over on the ridge, anyway, and it was all kind of glinted up with yellow up there, and it was getting more that way all the time. I was glad we were going up there, you can bet.

"What do you say we take a rest in the ferris-wheel?" Westy said. "It's just about in our path."

"Suits me," I said.

Now I'll tell you the way that wheel was. There were six cars and one of them was exactly at the top and one of them was exactly at the bottom. The trestle that the wheel hung on was only half as high as the wheel. Up near the top of the trestle was the axle. So as we came along in the same direction that the wheel was standing, the next car to the one on the bottom was right in front of us and hanging just about low enough so we could reach it. Those cars were not so big and they were boarded up just like everything else was in that old park.

Maybe you'll say that the easiest thing would have been for us to climb into the lowest car which was hanging right plunk underneath. But that one seemed to be all boarded up tight. Besides, my patrol is crazy, just as I told you. The next car on the side of the wheel nearer to us was partly open on account of the boards being broken away. So what did Westy do but take a running jump with the rest of us all after him. As soon as three or four of us grabbed hold of the car, the old wheel began creaking and the car started moving down. Then all of us went sprawling out all over the ground.

"Try it again!" the kid shouted. "One — two — —"

"Wait till it stops," they all shouted.

I can't tell you how far around that wheel went before it stopped. All I know is it kept creaking and creaking and then it stopped and there was a car right in front of us about ten feet from the ground. That one was most all open so it would be easy to tumble into it.

"One — two — three — go!" somebody said, and off we went for a good running jump.

I don't know who the first one was to catch hold of the car. But anyway, we all went tumbling over each other into it and down it went, creaking, creaking, creaking, till it hung from the lowest part of the wheel.

"All the comforts of home," Westy said. "I like this better than our private railroad car."

"Sure," I said, "it's just the place for Pee-wee; he's always going up in the air. Notice how it rocks? Oh, boy, I hope we don't get seasick."

In that car were two seats facing each other. Those cars were not made for as many as nine people, but we managed to crowd in all right. The floor of our car was about two or three feet from the ground and it swung like a swing. It was nice in there. Looking up through all the wire-work we could see the car at the top swinging.

"I'd like to be in that one," one of the fellows said.

"If you were in that one it would be this one," I told him.

"What are you talking about?" Pee-wee said.

"I'm talking about whether anything can be something else," I told him.

He said, "I suppose that's what you call mental digestion."

"It's logic," I told him. "If we were in that car, the nine of us, it would come down here, wouldn't it? Don't you know what the attraction of gravity is?"

"It never attracted me," he said.

"The heaviest part of a thing goes down," I said. "If you were up there you'd only come down here. The top car is the bottom one. Everything is something different.Up means where you're not. See? What do we care?"

We all sat there with our heads thrown back looking at the car away up above us.

"See how it rocks?" Dorry said. "I bet it's good and breezy up there."

"Why don't the others rock?" Hunt asked.

"Search me," I said.

"There's nothing on either side of that one at the top," Westy said. "There isn't even much of the wheel up there to break the force of the wind."

"Correct," I said. "Take two credits — and one cookie. Here."

"There isn't any such thing as the top of a wheel," Dorry said.

"Sure there is," I told him; "the part that's at the top is the top."

"The part that's at the top of what?" he came back at me.

"I should worry," I said. "Don't you think I've got wheels enough in my head without bothering about a ferris-wheel?"

So then we all started singing that crazy song that we used to sing when we were being hauled all over the country in our camp on wheels:

"There was a Duke of Yorkshire,He had ten thousand men;He marched them up the hill,And then he marched them down again.And when they're up, they're up,And when they're down, they're down;And when they're only half way up,They're neither up nor down."

CHAPTER XIX
UP IN THE AIR

It was nice in there.

"This is a good place to hide after killing a bandit," Warde Hollister said.

"Look out, you'll strain your neck," I said to Dorry, because he was craning his neck looking up.

He said, "I'm trying to decide which car is the one that was at the bottom when we came along. I think it's that one up top."

"They're all the same, only different," I said.

He said, "If I'm right it means that the wheel went just half way around—one half a revolution."

"Some highbrow," I said. "Don't talk about revolutions, they remind me of history. A half a revolution is better than the French Revolution. Take your feet off me. Do you want a whole car to yourself?"

"It's pretty crowded in here," Westy said.

"Well, go up on the top floor if you're not satisfied," I told him. "You'll get a good view up there."

"How do you know there's a good view in that car?" Pee-wee said.

"I put it in there when the car was down here," I told him. "Ask me something hard. Stop rocking, you make me dizzy."

Of course as soon as I said that they all started rocking the car. That shows how they obey their patrol leader. The car went swinging more and more and the rusty old wheel creaked.

"Git—app, git—appTill papa comes home,"

they started singing. Warde Hollister was as bad as any of them, if not worse.

"Have a heart," I said. "Stop! What is this? A life on the ocean wave or a bee-line hike?"

"Rock-a-bye babyOn the tree top,"

they all went on. Honest, that patrol is the limit. I'd like to sell it second-hand and get a new one.

"Listen to the ghosts up there," Westy said. "This old wheel sounds like a nineteen-sixteen Ford."

I said, "You'll look like a nineteen-sixteen Ford in a minute if you don't let up. Take that phonograph horn off my head," I said to Pee-wee; "or I'll throw it out of the car."

Pee-wee started yelling through it, "Only ten cents a ride on the haunted ferris-wheel. A—ll aboard! Only a dime, ten cents!"

We were all shaking, and our heads were wobbling and we were wiping our feet all over each other and the kid was shouting through his crazy megaphone, and I was just going to pull it away from him and throw it out of the car, when all of a sudden he dropped it and whispered, "Look— look! Up there! Look, quick!"

"You're seeing stars," I said; "no wonder."

"Look!" he said. "It's a—it's th—th——"

"Now you see what you get from swinging too much," I said.

"Look—athe—athe—uppp——" he stuttered. "I—sa—thbandidt——"

"No, you don't," I said. "No more bandits. Stop rocking, you fellows, will you; or this kid will be seeing some wild Indians."

They didn't pay any attention, only went on rocking the car more and more. They had been rocking so hard they couldn't stop. Pee-wee's jack-knife was bobbing against his belt, his compass was flopping around, his megaphone was all over our laps, and his cooking set was banging around on the floor. He was pointing up in the air the best he could and saying, "Stpthe car, stpthecar — ts — the bandit — tsthba — a — a — a — a — nt — —"

The more I laughed the dizzier I got and the dizzier I got the more I laughed. They were all laughing so hard and they were all so dizzy they couldn't speak.

"Atta — b — b — oy, kid!" one of them said.

Pee-wee was tumbling all around from one fellow's lap to another's and trying to talk. "Lkthba — a — a — a — a — nt — —" That was about all I could make of it.

CHAPTER XX

SEEING THINGS

Just then, I don't know, I seemed to see a face. I didn't know where I saw it but it was up above me.

I shouted, "Stop — op — op — this car — rar — I com — mom — mom — and you!"

Pretty soon the car stopped rocking.

"It's — it's the bandit," Pee-wee said; "did you see?"

"You've been seeing things," Westy said.

"I'll leave it to Roy," the kid said.

"I saw a face," I told them; "it was — —"

"Shh — look!" Pee-wee whispered; "straight up."

I looked, and away up through all the trestle work, I could see a head move back into the car at the top. The big axle of the wheel was right between our car and that other one and it hid part of the car. It seemed as if that person up there had been peeking at us and drew in his head quickly so as not to be seen. I saw this much, that he had a cap on.

"Did you see?" I whispered to Westy.

"Sure I did," he said. "That was no baseball target."

"Baseball target?" the kid whispered, all excited. "That's the bandit; now we've got him."

Dorry said, "Don't look up again; don't let him think we saw him. He had a cap on. Did you see?"

"I suppose I'll have to climb up there and shoot him," Warde Hollister said.

"You sit where you are," I told him. I knew he was only joking but I saw that was no time for fooling and I was afraid he might spoil everything.

"You could never climb up there," I said. "Anyway, this is no false alarm. I saw him as plain as day."

"So did I," Westy whispered. Hunt and Will said they thought they had seen him too, but they weren't sure because they had been seeing everything on account of being so dizzy.

Westy said, "Don't talk loud, remember sound ascends."

I made believe I was looking all around at the sky and I stole a look up that way again. Just as I did I saw a kind of a movement. I kind of knew that the person away up there in that car was watching us and sticking his head out as much as he dared.

Westy said, "We don't know whether it's the bandit or not, but whoever it is, we've got him. He'd break his neck jumping from up there. He couldn't get hold of the trestle on either side of the car. That car must have been down here when we came along. Whoever it is, we've got him as sure as if we had handcuffs on him."

"We've foiled him," the kid whispered. "You said boys never capture bandits and things except in books. Now you see."

Westy said, "Well, we've sure got him, and believe me, that's a new way to capture a bandit."

"It shows that scouts are resourceful," Pee-wee said.

I said, "Sure, they're so resourceful they capture bandits without knowing it. We don't even know if he is a bandit."

"We know we've got him. Isn't that enough?" the kid said.

Jiminies, whoever he was, I could see we had him all right. He was as safe up there as he would have been in a dungeon. Because you can see how it was. The big tall trestle-work that held the axle was only as high as the middle of the wheel. Maybe he could have climbed down that, and maybe he couldn't. But from the middle of the wheel up to the top the iron-work wasn't close enough for him to reach from one brace to another. I didn't see how he could even get out of the car to the nearest girder. If he took a chance, he'd break his neck. I suppose, just like Westy said, he had made for the lowest car and it had gone up with him on account of our weight hanging onto some of the other cars. Nine fellows are heavier than one. Gee whiz, it did seem a funny way to catch any one, but that fellow was caught, sure. I wondered how he felt up there.

"Do you think he'll take a chance of his life?" one of the fellows asked.

"I bet he's half crazy up there," I said.

"Maybe he'll shoot," the kid said, kind of scared.

"What good would that do him?" Will said. "He'd have to shoot the whole nine of us, six or seven of us anyway, before the wheel would move. And besides, the axle is in his way."

"If we all leave here the car will come down," Warde Hollister said. "He could rock it so as to get the wheel started."

"It's rocking a little now," Westy said.

"I know what I'm going to do," I told them. "I'm going to find out who he is, if I can."

"You're not going to go up and ask him!" the kid said. "You might better use the megaphone. Safety first."

I said, "I'm going to make believe I'm hunting for something and see if there are any footprints around. If there are and they're from the direction of the river, that will look bad."

On the fancy seats were four wooden knobs, two on each seat. I said, "Turn one of those and see if it screws off."

Warde was sitting at the end of one of the seats and he kept turning the knob till it came off.

I said, "Reach down under your knees — don't anybody look up — reach down under your knees and wrap your handkerchief tight around that knob, so it will look like a baseball or a tennis ball. Then throw it over here."

The paint was all gone from those knobs and the wood was all cracked and rotten like all the wood in that old park. I wanted the ball to look white so it would be good and plain to the fellow up there.

In a few seconds Warde and I began throwing it to each other. No one would be suspicious seeing us, that's sure. Pretty soon I threw it good and hard, like Christy Matthewson, only different, and it went flying out in the direction of the river and dropped. It went in the long grass.

And then is when I had good luck. Because I didn't have to go five feet from that car before I found something. So you see I didn't get off the track of our bee-line enough to really call it getting off the track.

I made believe I was hunting for the ball, and in about ten seconds, good night, right there near the car were footprints. I could see them as plain as day. They came from the direction of the river, too. Not in a bee-line the way we had come. But just the same they came from the river, all right.

"I can't find the pesky old ball," I shouted. "Why don't you throw straight when you're throwing? Come on, let's go to Little Valley and get some ice cream cones. We should worry."

"I like this old car," Westy shouted. "If we leave it maybe the wind will carry it up. Let's tie it with our rope and come back here and eat our supper in it on the way home. After that it can spin around till it gets dizzy for all we care. Wha'd' you say?"

I could just hear him saying, "Shhh," to the other fellows.

That's Westy Martin all over; he always has his wits about him. I'd carry mine around with me, too, if I had any, only I haven't got any. Sometimes Pee-wee has good ideas, but he doesn't carry them with him because he has so much else to carry. But Westy has a dandy brain, I'll say that for him. I saw right away what he was driving at.

"That's a crackerjack idea," I shouted. "Let's eat our supper here on the way back. We'll tie the car and then we can loosen it again afterwards. Come on, let's hurry up. This is a nice lonely place to eat in and nobody anywhere around to bother us."

"Hurrah!" they all shouted.

CHAPTER XXI
FETTERS

So that's the way we did. As we went away we were all careful not to look up, and we talked about all different things as if we didn't know there was any one up in that wheel at all. And if anybody ever tells you that boy scouts can't really catch grown-up people except in books, you can tell them I said they can do it in amusement parks too.

"I hope he's the highwayman, anyway," I said to Pee-wee. "You're not the only one that goes up in the air."

"It shows what scouts can do," Pee-wee said. "We bound him with ropes, didn't we?"

"Absolutely," I said, "only the rope was quite a way off from him."

"What difference does that make?" he wanted to know. "He's held by ropes, isn't he? Can you deny that?"

"I guess you're right," Westy laughed.

"What are we going to do now?" Hunt wanted to know.

"We're going to keep our eyes on that tree," I said, "and go in a bee-line. It will take more than an auto bandit to get me off the straight path. Don't look back whatever you do."

I guess it was about five o'clock then; anyway it must have been after four because we were getting hungry. It's strenuous work catching bandits. The tree up on the ridge was all kind of red. The sky was bright over there and it looked fine. That's the time I like best, when the sun begins to get red. I was wondering if we could see my house when we got up on the ridge.

Pretty soon we climbed over the old amusement park fence and then we just had to cut straight across fields till we came to Little Valley. Before we got there all the windows in the houses looked as if there were lights shining inside of them. That was a sign the sun was beginning to go down. When the windows look bright like that in August you'll know it's after five o'clock. In Bridgeboro at six o'clock some of the houses in Little Valley look as if they were on fire. We got fooled that way once. We went all the way there by the road and there wasn't any building burning down at all. Gee whiz, we were mad!

Little Valley isn't so big. The fellows over there come to Bridgeboro High School. There's a one-patrol troop there. Harry Donnelle lives there too. He told us whenever we came to Little Valley to be quiet so as not to wake the people up. He says that place ought to be called Rip Van Winkleberg. But anyway, I don't see how you can wake a town up if it's dead. The only thing that's quick about Little Valley is some quicksand near the creek. But they've got a good ball field there for the Bridgeboro team to beat them on. Anyway, I'm not so stuck on baseball. Me for stalking and tracking and all that.

Now when we got to Little Valley we marched in formation just the same as we did in Bridgeboro, two rows of three fellows each. I marched ahead with my official staff and we let Warde Hollister go ahead of us all with the cardboard standard because he didn't have any scout suit. I bet Little Valley felt like Belgium when it saw us coming.

We had to go across one lawn, but a lady told us it was all right. Pee-wee started to give her a lecture about the scouts but I grabbed him by the collar and made him come along. He rattled like an old junk wagon. The lady said he looked like Don Quixote. I don't know much about that fellow, but if I ever meet him I'm going to apologize to him for what she said.

Next we came to Main Street, named after the water main. By that time we had a crowd of kids at our heels again and everybody was staring at us. I hope they liked us. A man let us go through his store and climb over the back fence and then we came out on the village green.

There's a band-stand on that village green and a whole crowd of kids climbed up into it so as to see us. Pee-wee looked mighty proud. A lot of grown people were standing around too, staring at us and laughing. I guess they thought our big sign looked pretty funny.

One man said, "Is the civilian population going to be spared?"

I said, "The civilized population is going to be spared, but if there are any ice cream cones in this berg they're going to die a horrible death. Plant our banner in the village green," I said to Warde, "and all gather around your gallant leader."

The man said, "How do you feel about peanut brittle?"

"No peanut brittle can get past us," I told him. "We eat it alive."

Oh, boy, there was some excitement. The next thing we knew a box of peanut brittle was going round. There was a crowd of people all around watching and reading what it said on our standard and laughing. Most always that's the way it is with people when they see scouts. Somebody kicked a grocery box over to where we were and the man called, "Speech, speech." I got up on the box and I said:

"Don't anybody be afraid, we're not going to hurt you."

A girl that was standing there said, "The idea! Did you ever hear of such a thing? Hurt us? Do you think we're afraid of a patrol of boy scouts?"

I said, "You knowest not what thou sayest, girl. We've devastated the whole country from Blakeley's Hill to this spot. The only thing we've left alive is the grass. And even that we trod under our feet."

"We're invincible!" Pee-wee shouted. "Do you know what that is?"

"Do you think I haven't got a dictionary, Mr. Smarty?" she said.

I said, "Silence. Take a demerit. Where is the police department of this town?"

Somebody shouted, "He's home eating his supper. Do you want to go and see him?"

I said, "No, we want him to come and see us. Can't you see from our sign we're on a bee-line hike?"

Somebody shouted, "He's at supper. Do you have to see him?"

I said, "No, the army and navy will do just as well; we're not particular. Wait till I consult with my official staff."

I couldn't understand what my official staff said because his mouth was full of peanut brittle. "Here's the box, eat that too," I said.

Then I said good and loud, "We have an important communication to address to the police department. We've caught a bandit — —"

"We've got him bound with fetters," the kid shouted.

"Give me that phonograph horn," I told him; "the crowd is growing bigger."

Good night, that was the end of me. I was superseded like a general in the third grade—I mean in history. There was Pee-wee standing on the grocery box, his aluminum cooking set all over the ground, shouting through the old phonograph horn at the top of his voice. A little way off I could see a cop coming across the green. I guess he was going to chase us off first, till he heard what Pee-wee was saying.

CHAPTER XXII
INVASION

Pee-wee had the floor; he had the whole green; I guess he had nearly the whole town. Anyway, he had all the peanut brittle there was left.

"We caught a bandit," he shouted. "He's got footprints. He's up in the top car of the ferris-wheel in Riverview Park. He's bound with ropes. Even Detective Pinchem didn't catch him, but we did."

"Who put him up there?" somebody shouted.

"We did!" Pee-wee yelled.

"What's he doing up there?" a man called.

"He's trembling with fear," the kid shouted. "He fired seven hundred shots and got away with two dollars — — "

"You mean seven hundred dollars," I said.

"We foiled him!" the kid shouted.

"He's all wrapped up in tin-foil," I said.

The cop said, "What's all this nonsense, anyway?"

I said, "Are you the police department?"

He said, "Well, I think I am."

"You've got to be sure of it," Pee-wee shouted. "We can't deal with the civilized population."

"Do you think we're afraid of you?" that girl said, very scornful like.

"Hurrah for Pee-wee Harris," Dorry shouted.

"Do you think we're afraid of a boy named Pee-wee?" she said. "It sounds like a canary bird."

Pee-wee pointed the big horn right plunk at her and shouted through it, "Do you call me a canary bird?"

I nearly died laughing.

She said, "If I had a name like Pee-wee I wouldn't talk about dealing with the civilian population."

"That name doesn't belong to me," he yelled.

"He only rents it," Hunt said.

"His right name is Sir Harris, R. R. — Raving Raven," Dorry said.

"What's your name?" Pee-wee hollered at her through the horn.

"It's Dora Dane Daring," she said. "So there, Mr. Smarty. And I'm a girl scout."

"Girls are afraid of snakes," he shouted.

She said, "Well, they're not afraid of canary birds."

"They're afraid of black men and — and — bandits," he yelled. "Didn't you ever hear of wild canary birds? That shows how much you know about botany — I mean zoology."

By that time everybody was screaming. Even the whole police department was laughing. He said, "Well, now, what's all this about? Have you youngsters been dreaming or what?"

"What," I said; "you guessed right the second time."

I guess if it hadn't been for Westy maybe that fellow with the cap would be up on the top of the wheel yet.

He said to the policeman, "I'll tell you how it was if these fellows will keep still."

I said, "Let's have a large chunk of silence."

So then Westy told him all about our meeting Detective Pinchem and how he was looking for a fellow that had robbed an auto party and how he had stolen a boat and left it in the marshes. He told him all about what happened at the old ferris-wheel and how I had found footprints there and how they showed that some one had come from the river. Most all the people that crowded around listening were serious. Two or three men said they guessed it was the auto bandit all right. The policeman said they'd soon find out.

A lot of people said they were going to see what happened and one or two of the patrol wanted to go back because, one thing, you don't see bandits captured every day. Maybe whole weeks might go by and you'd never see one captured in a ferris-wheel. But that shows how you never can tell. You might chase a bandit on a merry-go-round but you'd never catch him.

"We should worry about the bandit," that's what I told the fellows. "Because we've got troubles of our own. We've got to make Carson's Hill yet and then the woods up the ridge and we'll have to go slow and use our compass in there. Look at that big tree up there waiting for us," I said. "It's got all dressed up for us since we started."

And, honest, it did look that way because it was all gold. But, anyway, you'll find out in the next chapter that gold isn't the only color. There are blue and green and yellow and strawberry and orange and banana and grape-fruit and peaches and russet apples — those are my favorites. Gee whiz, I don't know whether I'm talking about fruit or colors! But one kind of vegetable I like, and that is onions.

Anyway, the color I was going to speak about is black. And believe me the next chapter is the darkest one in this book.

CHAPTER XXIII
FOILED!

Most of the people went back to the park with the police department. That girl had been listening to Westy telling the policeman about everything and so now she said to our young hero:

"You don't call that binding a bandit with ropes, do you? With him up at the top of the wheel and you down at the bottom."

The kid said, "Sure I do, that's distance binding—you're so smart. That shows how much you know about scouting. I suppose you don't know you can signal for miles and miles. Can't you do other things by distance too?"

"That's a fine argument," Warde Hollister said.

"I invented it," the kid shouted.

That girl said, very sarcastic like, "I must say you were very brave to kill that wooden figure. I'm not afraid of snakes, but I'd certainly be afraid of a wooden figure. Tell me, did you ever kill a rag doll?"

There were two or three girl friends of hers there and they all started to titter.

"Was it our fault if that colored man was made of wood?" Pee-wee said.

She said, "Oh, mercy, no. But when you were binding the poor bandit weren't you afraid he'd bite you? He was only a hundred feet or so away, you know. Are you afraid of mice, too?"

"No, we're not afraid of mice," Pee-wee said. "And we're not afraid of bugs either. Girls are afraid of June bugs."

"That's because they're black," she said.

"Scouts aren't afraid of anything, they don't care what color it is——"

"Purple or lavender or pale white or dark black, what do we care?" I said.

"Do you see that hill away over there in the east?" the kid shouted at her. "That's Blakeley's Hill. That's miles away. We came from there in a bee-line. Do you think that we let anything stand in our way? We're—we're—invincible. Houses—we go right through them. Even the movie people followed us, so now you can tell. Rivers—do you think that river stopped us? Do you know what the points of the compass are? We came straight west, just as straight as an arrow. Now we're going up on that ridge, where that big tree is. If you want to follow us, you can. Then you can see just how we do it. You'll see us—you'll see us go right through houses. I'm not blaming girls that they don't have adventures——"

She said, "Oh, isn't that too sweet?"

"And who are you going to kill next?" another one of those girls wanted to know. "Some terrible black man?"

"The blacker the better," I said.

"Do you see that tree off there on the ridge?" Pee-wee asked her. "We have to climb right up that. There are snakes up there."

She said, "Oh, isn't that terrible?"

"I'm not saying you can't do things," the kid said; "because girls know how to sew and cook, I have to admit that. But when it comes to——"

"To being invincible?" she said.

"Now you just shut one eye and look at that big tree up there," Pee-wee said. "Do you notice the house right at the edge of this green? Do you see how it's right in a bee-line with that tree? We've got to go right through that house. Do you think we'd go around it? We'll go right plunk through the middle of it, no matter what. That's what a bee-line hike means. That's why we had the police department come to us instead of our going to him. See?"

All the girls began to laugh. Dora Dane Daring said, "Isn't that just wonderful?"

"That's nothing," Pee-wee said. "We do harder things than that."

They all began to laugh again.

I said, "Well, as long as we can't take this village with us we'll have to leave it here, I suppose. I hope it will be here when we get back."

"Maybe if you bound it with ropes — —" one of those girls said.

"It would just be a waste of good rope," I said. "We'll stand a rock on the town and that will hold it here. Come on, official staff," I said, "get busy. You fellows fall into line. The next assault is on that house that Pee-wee pointed out. Am I right?"

They all lined it up with the tree so as to make sure.

"Now you watch us," I said to the girls.

"Oh, we'll watch you," one of them said. Then they all began to laugh again.

I said, "If you have patrols in the Girl Scouts, yours ought to be called the Laughing Hyenas. What's the idea?"

They didn't answer, only just stood there giggling. They ought to have a merit badge for giggling in the Girl Scouts.

"We think you're so funny," one of them said; "especially that little boy."

"Your village isn't so big if it comes to that," Pee-wee said.

"No, but it hasn't got coffee-pots and frying pans and old phonographs hanging all over it," one of them said, laughing all the while. "He looks like an ash wagon."

"That shows how much you know about scouting," the kid shouted. "Don't you know that scouts are supposed to cook their own meals?"

"And play their own music?" Dora Dane Daring said. "Do you take victrola lessons?"

I said, "He plays the shoe horn, also the gas pipe. He can even play on Boys' Life; that's the scouts' official organ."

She said, "Most canary birds are musical."

"Yes," I said, "and parrots can laugh, too."

She said, "You ought to call it an A. B. C. hike instead of a B hike. If you're going to tear down any houses we'd like to see you do it."

"Everybody falls for the scouts — in all the houses," Pee-wee yelled.

That Daring girl just giggled and said, "Oh, isn't that just wonderful?"

So then I rounded up my army of invasion and I shouted, "Scouts and sprouts, I have squinted yonder tree with my trusty right eye and I find we have to cross neutral territory again. We have to go through that house over there — —"

"The one with the roof of — —" Pee-wee shouted.

I said, "That's the one, the one with the roof. Take a good look at that house; you'll see it has an inside as well as an outside."

"I can't see the inside," Dorry shouted.

"Can you see the outside?" I asked him. "Well, the inside is just inside of the outside. If you took the outside away there wouldn't be any inside. You can do that by algebra."

I said, "There are two stories in that house and we have to put some adventure into those stories."

Pee-wee shouted, "I'll go ahead and ring the bell and tell them we want to go through, hey? Because I know what to say." Then he said to the girls, "You can watch me if you want to. Maybe some time you'll be on a bee-line hike and want to go through a house and then you'll know just how to do."

One of them said, "Oh, thank you so much."

"The pleasure is ours," I told her. "If the civilized population wants to follow us, what do we care?"

Then I said, "Ready — go!"

We all marched across the green with Pee-wee ahead of us and those girls coming along behind, laughing. You couldn't blame them because the kid looked awfulfunny — very brave and bold. We all stopped on the walk in front of the house. It was a dandy big house; it looked like one of those houses that has a hall running straight through to the back. That's the kind of neutral territory I like.

The kid marched straight up to the steps and up onto the porch and pushed the button. "That's one thing you have to learn when you're a scout," he called down, "not to be afraid."

All of a sudden the front door opened and, g-o-o-d night, magnolia! There was the biggest colored man I ever saw. He was about six feet tall and eight feet in circumference, or maybe it was the other way round, I don't know which. His face was so black that it would make a blackboard look pale. You could have written on that man's face with chalk, dandy. He had on a kind of a uniform with brass buttons and his elbows stuck out on each side of him.

"Good night," Hunt said; "that's one mountain we didn't figure on."

I said, "I guess that's one of the Black Hills. I wonder how it got out of my geography."

Pee-wee looked like a kewpie doll in front of that man. The man just glared at him and then he said, good and loud, "Whatchue want here, you?"

Pee-wee said, "We—eh—we—does Mr. Smith live here—please?"

The big man said, "No, he don't. Whatchue want here?" He just glared down at the poor kid as if he were going to eat him.

Pee-wee said, kind of hesitating, "If—if we'd be willing to wipe our feet—maybe—would you be willing to let us go through this house—maybe?"

The big man glared down at him and then he said in a great big deep voice, "Looker here, you youngster! You want to get arrested, do you? You clear out of this!Whatchue mean comin' to folks' houses and say you like to go through, eh? You clear out of here, double quick, or I'll have you in de lockup!"

80

He banged the door shut and there stood Pee-wee trying to get his breath, I guess. Then he started down the steps again, the stuff in his big megaphone rattling like a junk wagon.

"Foiled!" I said.

CHAPTER XXIV
DARING DORA DANE

Oh, boy, you should have heard those girls laugh. Dora Dane Daring said, "Isn't that just too provoking? He didn't seem to be a bit afraid of you, did he?"

"Don't you know sometimes scouts have to use strategy?" Pee-wee said. "Did you think I was going to—to—just force my way in? Don't you know a scout has to be courteous?"

"It was so good of you not to hurt him," she said.

"Scouts are—they're kind," the kid said.

She said, "Yes, but you know they're invincible. I suppose you'll just go and ring the bell again?"

"We—we take turns doing things like that," the kid said.

"The general appoints scouts to do that," I told her. "I appoint Westy Martin and Dorry Benton to——"

"I can't be drafted, I have a dependent ancestor," Dorry said.

Westy said, "I'm sorry, but I have heart trouble. I claim exemption."

I said, "You're a fine pair. I appoint Will Dawson and Warde Hollister to go up there and arrange terms——"

Warde said, "I'm sorry, but I'm not in uniform."

"I have a dependent mother," Will Dawson said.

"I'm a conscientious objector," Hunt Manners piped up.

The Warner twins said they were the sole support of a collie dog.

"Some bunch of warriors," I said. "I always heard that scouts weren't supposed to be afraid of a draught. What are we going to do? Go home?"

"If we had tanks——" the kid started.

"Well, go and get a couple of water tanks," I said.

"Isn't it exasperating?" one of the girls said.

"Can't you wait a little while?" Pee-wee shouted. "Wasn't the world war four years long? That shows what you know about history."

One of the girls said, "Do you still claim to be invincible?"

"Sure we do," Pee-wee said. "But of course everybody—a lot of people know that women helped in the war a lot—everybody knows that. We wouldn't be mad if you made a suggestion."

That Daring girl said, "Oh, I haven't a single thing to suggest. We believe in action. Actions speak louder than suggestions. If you're really ready to admit that you're defeated I'll make a proposal. It isn't a suggestion, it's a proposal."

"Proposals are just as good as suggestions," Pee-wee said.

She said, "Well, if you're ready to admit that you're balked——"

"Even—even—even the Germans were balked on the Marne, weren't they?" our young hero shouted.

I said, "Well, it doesn't look as if that giant with the brass buttons is going to surrender. If we could get some propaganda past him to the people in the house——"

"Like they did with airplanes," Pee-wee said.

"Yes, but you see the shutters are closed," she said. "Girl scouts are observant. It looks as if there were no one in the house but that horrid big giant."

I said, "What do you propose?"

Then Dora Dane Daring said, "I propose to lead you to victory if you will print it up on your banner that you were saved from disaster by the Girl Scouts of America, and keep that on your banner till you get home."

"I'd like to see you do it first," I said.

"You mean to tell me you're not afraid of that man?" Pee-wee said. "Do you think I'd let you—a scout has to be chivalrous. He has to protect women——"

"Give me your hatchet," she said, and she jerked it out of his belt.

"You better look out what you're doing," the kid said. "Do you want to get arrested?"

She swung Pee-wee's belt-axe in the air just like Carrie Nation or Joan of Arc and she said, "Follow me!"

Pee-wee said, "Dora Dane Daring, you'd better look out what you're doing."

She said, "Private Canary Bird Harris, you're a coward. Fall in line, everybody!"

Gee whiz, I thought that girl was crazy. Up she marched, right onto the porch, with all the rest of us after her. Pee-wee kind of hung back—safety first for him. I was ready to run any minute. We went across that porch as if we were stalking a bird.

But she didn't care. She just hit the door a good rap with the hatchet and kept pushing the button. Boy, I was kind of shaky!

Pee-wee said to her, "You'd better be ready to run."

I said, "I'm ready to go scout-pace for ten miles. I'm glad a scout can run."

I guess that big army all rolled into one with the brass buttons must have known it was our crowd because he didn't come right away. Gee whiz, I pictured him getting madder and madder every second. I was ready to jump from the porch to the middle of the street. Pee-wee had one leg all ready for a good starter. All the while Dora Dane Daring kept pounding on the door and pushing the button.

All of a sudden the door opened. That's the end of this chapter.

CHAPTER XXV
PEE-WEE'S LOSS

Pee-wee gave a sudden start, then stopped. We all kind of stood back a little. Westy and Dorry stayed by the railing. We were all ready to retreat in disorder. There was that great big man filling up the whole doorway and his brass buttons shining. He looked like the Allied Army. She just shouted right in his face,

"Stand aside and let these boys pass, in the name of the Girl Scouts of America!"

G-o-o-d night, as sure as I'm writing this, that great big colored man stood out of the way and in she marched waving Pee-wee's belt-axe. We all followed after her, kind of scary.

"You'd—you'd better look out," Pee-wee whispered to her. "He can lock us in here and have us all arrested. Maybe—you can't tell—maybe he meditates treachery.What—what are you going to do?"

"We're going to devastate his country, Private Canary Bird Pee-wee," she said. "Now you see what the Girl Scouts of America can do. Maybe sometime you'll want to know how to break through hostile territory and then you'll remember Dora Dane Daring, won't you? Do you think I'm afraid of a butler?"

"You'd—you'd better look out," Pee-wee said; "safety first."

As we went through the hall he kept looking all around as if he expected to see sharpshooters behind all the doors. It was a dandy house, with a nice big wide hall and it had a moose's head for a hat rack. First I guess we were all pretty scared.

The kid walked on tiptoe through the hall, and he kept whispering to me, "This is just like—it's just like burglary. Girls are reckless. We'd better look out. Do you hear a footstep upstairs? I hear a bell ringing. I bet he's calling up the police, hey?"

That girl led the way into a dandy big dining room and then all her friends began laughing again.

She said, "We'll take everything there is to eat in the pantry. My brave army must be fed."

Pee-wee said, "I'm — I'm not so hungry." Gee whiz, it was the first time I ever heard him admit that.

She said, "If there is any bird seed in this house you shall have it. Sit down."

Pee-wee sat down on the edge of a chair, looking all around, good and scared. Every time a door creaked he gave a start. He said, "It's — it's in — it says in the scout handbook that we have no right to trespass — — "

She waved the belt-axe and she said, "The scout handbook! Ho, ho! A mere scrap of paper." She was awful funny.

Pee-wee said, "We didn't mean to stay here. All we wanted was to go through — — "

"Do you eat pie?" she said.

He said, "Yes, but — maybe we'd better start."

We were all sitting around the dining room. I guess all of us felt kind of shaky. I thought every minute that Pee-wee was going to get up and run.

All of a sudden Westy (gee, he's a fiend for noticing things) — he said, "Dora Dane Daring, the boy scouts have to hand it to you; you've done a good turn, that's sure. This house looked like a hard proposition. All we have to do now is climb over that fence in back. We all admit you're a heroine. But there's one thing I'd like to ask you. Do you notice that big silver cup on the sideboard has D D D engraved on it? Maybe scouts aren't so much as warriors but they're observant. I was wondering if you know whose initials those are?"

At that all the girls started laughing.

"It's your own house!" Pee-wee shouted. "Now you see how scouts are observant. What did I tell you?"

She said, "It is not my own house; so there, Mr. Canary Bird Harris."

"Whose house is it?" Westy said.

"It's my father's, Mr. Smarty," she said.

"No sooner said than stung," I told Westy.

Hunt said, "What difference does it make whose house it is as long as we go through it? We have to give you the credit anyway."

"Is your father home?" Warde asked her.

She said, "Nobody's home but myself — and the butler."

I said, "Yes, I seem to remember him. I think Pee-wee met him once."

"I — I found out that I'm — kind of — that I'm hungrier than I thought I was," the kid said.

"Oh, sure," I said; "his appetite is like a cat, it always comes back."

And believe me, that was the only time in the life of P. Harris that I ever knew him to lose his appetite. Even then it was only for four minutes. Westy said it was three minutes and a half, but what's the difference?

He got it back anyway.

CHAPTER XXVI
THE SHERO

One thing about scouts—I mean two things about them. They always keep their words and they always keep their appetites—you can ask anybody.

I said, "Bring down a bottle of shoe-blacking with a sponge brush and we'll let the whole World know that you're a hero, I mean a shero."

She said, "First we're going to have refreshments."

I said, "No, first we're going to give you credit."

She just laughed and she said, "No, because it's my father's house."

I said, "That's not your fault. If that butler was in my house he'd scare the life out of me just the same. I hope you never feed him meat. Even if I met him at the Peace Conference he'd scare me."

So two or three of those girls went upstairs and got a bottle of shoe blacking and a big piece of cardboard. It was the cover of a box a suit comes in. I printed on it good and plain:

WITH THE ASSISTANCE

OF

THE GIRL SCOUTS

and we fastened that just underneath the other sign on our martial standard. Pee-wee kind of balked at that.

But he didn't balk at eating pie. They had dandy pie in that house. We all sat around the dining room eating refreshments and we had a good time. Pee-wee showed them that a scout could eat, anyway. Even still, every time there was a noise he gave a start. Safety first.

Dora Dane Daring said she liked Bridgeboro.

Pee-wee said, "Were you ever in Bennett's there?"

She said no, but she knew some girls there.

I said, "Do you know Minerva Skybrow? We named a kind of mushroom after her."

She said, "The idea!"

I said, "It's a good idea; she showed us all about how to grow mushrooms. She can play tennis in four languages, that girl can. There are a lot of smart people in Bridgeboro. We've got three patrols in our troop but, thank goodness, there's only one of them here. That's enough, hey?"

Westy said, "If you ever come on a hike to Bridgeboro — — "

"Maybe you can't walk that far," Pee-wee said.

She just looked at him, very scornful.

I said, "If you ever come over there, come and see us in our headquarters; we're away most of the time — I didn't mean it that way. — We've got a railroad car for a meeting-place down by the river. Drop in if you're ever down that way."

"Drop in the river?" she said. "Aren't you perfectly dreadful!"

"The river's all right," Pee-wee said.

One of the other girls said, "I bet you have lots of fun, you boys."

"We eat it alive," I told her. "There's a scarcity of fun in Bridgeboro because we used it all up. That's why we have to explore the country. The next thing we're going to do is a zigzag hike."

She said, "Did anybody ever tell you you were crazy?"

"Nobody has to tell us," I said, "because we know it. Anyway, I guess we have to be going now."

We had dandy fun sitting around there talking. Girls are all right, only they're kind of funny, they keep giggling all the time — giggling and fixing their hair. But anyway, they know how to do good turns. Most of them like algebra and they're funny in other ways too. But gee whiz, everybody has something the matter with him. I know a girl who stuck a safety pin on a stump for a scout sign. But they're strong on being kind and all that, I'll say that much.

Those girls took us out across the lawn in back and when I pointed out the big poplar tree away up there on west ridge they said they'd like to be going with us. And Dora Dane Daring said she was glad her father owned that house, so she could help us to keep to our bee-line. They stood there at the fence waving to us until we got away over pretty near to Westcott's Hill. One of them threw a kiss to us then. Girls always wait till you get far away before they do that so that you can't be really sure whether they meant it that way or not.

But I was sure, all right.

CHAPTER XXVII

THE NEW SCOUT

Now comes the part of our bee-line hike that I like best because we had to go through woods and open country. Houses and villages are all right, but me for the open country. There wasn't any one following us now, there were no buildings or anything like that ahead, and it seemed quiet and lonely. Up to that time our hike had been sort of like a circus, only more so. But pretty soon, oh, boy, it wasn't much like a circus, because something pretty serious happened.

It was beginning to get dusk by that time and there were kind of like little dabs of dark red on the top of the ridge. Away up on the peak of the big poplar tree was a dab of red and all the rest of it was dark. It seemed awful clear against the sky, that tree. I kind of thought how all day long the sun had been on a bee-line hike too, going straight west. "If the sun can do it, we can do it," that's what I said. It would be nice up there under that tree in the dusk. I was hoping that we'd get there soon so we could start a fire. Then my mother could see that from the porch and she'd know we were all right. Because we'd come back around by the road and that would be easy. We could take the jitney on the state road right up there on the ridge and go straight to Bridgeboro station. I don't know if you know where the Bridgeboro station is, but it's right near Bennett's.

Now I'll tell you about the country from Little Valley to west ridge. First it's easy, across fields. Then you come to Westcott's Hill. Gee whiz, I don't know what he ever wanted to own a hill like that for. The side nearest Little Valley isn't very steep but going down the other side it's pretty steep. On that side the hill is sort of broken off like. We weren't worrying because we knew there'd be some way down. We should worry about hills. At the foot of that hill is a deep cut where the railroad goes through. On the other side of the railroad tracks the ridge begins. Before you get to the ridge there's a pond—a pretty big one. Up the side of the ridge are woods.

Now most all the way from Little Valley to the ridge we could see the tree. There were only two places where we couldn't see it. One was just before we got to the hill. But after we got part way up the hill we could see it again. The other place was west of the hill, in the hollow. We knew how it would be there but we didn't care because we had our compass. We intended to go up through the woods on the ridge with our compass.

It was pretty easy going till we got up to the top of the hill but then we saw that it was going to be pretty hard getting down it, it was so steep. It went down a little way, maybe ten feet, almost straight. Then there was a kind of a little slanting shelf with all grass and bushes. We didn't know how it was below that slanting shelf because we couldn't see. Maybe it was so that we could climb down. If it wasn't it would have to be pretty steep.

So we stood on the top of the hill thinking what we would do.

Warde Hollister said, "The only thing to do is for one of us to climb down on that ledge and look over and see how steep it is below. Then we'll know whether we can make it or not. There's no use turning back till we know we have to."

"Turning back?" I said.

"Well, what else are we going to do if we can't get down this hill?" he wanted to know.

"All our day's hike for nothing?" Westy said.

"I didn't say I'm for turning back," Warde said. "But this isn't a case of ringing front door bells and getting on the right side of people. Maybe scouts like Nature, but Nature doesn't care much about scouts."

"You said something," I told him. "But, gee whiz, we don't want to turn back."

He said, "Well, there's no use crying till we're hurt. We've got to find out how steep it is below and that ought to be easy."

He started throwing off his jacket.

"Only you'd better be careful," I said. "That ledge is kind of slanting."

"It's all full of bushes," he said.

"How will you get up again if you have to come back?" one of the fellows asked him.

"A couple of you can reach down," he said. "There's a good foothold up on top here."

I didn't like the idea of his doing that. But I didn't like the idea of turning back either.

After leaving Little Valley I guess we had all begun to think it would be easy going on account of there not being any streets or houses in our way. Because, one thing, scouts are used to the open country. We never thought about running into anything like that. It came all of a sudden, like, and there we were with the big tree on the ridge across the valley, plain to see, and we couldn't seem to get any farther. Gee williger, it was pretty hard for any of us to think about turning back then, after going right straight for that tree all day long.

"I don't know about that," Westy said. He's always careful.

Warde said, "Well, what are we going to do then? Turn back? We could go north and down the hill where it's easy, but that wouldn't be a bee-line hike."

I said, "This is a bee-line hike; it's either straight west or home, victory or defeat. No beating around the bush."

"That's us!" they all shouted.

Warde said, "Well, then, we've either got to go on or turn back. And I'm going to find out which we have to do. There's no use standing here talking about it. If we're beaten, we might as well know it. We can be good losers, I hope. We can either go down this hill or we can't and I'm not going to say we can't till I know we can't. That's the kind of a scout I'm — going to be."

"You mean it's the kind of a scout you are," I told him. "And I'm glad to have you in my patrol, I'll tell you that!"

"Maybe this hill can beat me," he said; "but it can't fool me. Here, hold my jacket."

CHAPTER XXVIII
THE LEDGE

If it hadn't been for that slanting ledge a little below us we could have looked down and seen just how steep the hill was. It would be bad enough to have to turn back, anyway, that's what I thought. But to turn back without really knowing for sure that we couldn't possibly go any further, gee whiz, that didn't seem like scouts. We were all feeling pretty disappointed because we knew that the chances were against us.

"We'll either do it or know that we can't, that's our motto," Hunt said.

"And if we can't, that will mean no one can," I said.

"That's us," Dorry shouted.

"Give me a hand down," Warde said.

"A scout in khaki ought to do that," I said. "We ought not to let a new fellow risk — —"

"You're so strong on good turns," Warde said. "Aren't you willing to give a fellow a chance to win the khaki? Here, grab hold of my hand. I'm not going to walk off the ledge. Do you think I'm blind?"

"Well, anyway, be careful," I said. I felt kind of shaky, I couldn't help it. Because below that ledge there must have been a hundred feet and for all we knew it was straight up and down.

I got a good firm foothold by bracing my feet behind a rock. "Stand back," I said to the other fellows. Then I held Warde's hand while he climbed down onto the ledge. I couldn't keep hold of his hand till he got all the way down, but he braced his feet on the side of the rock that made a kind of wall up from the ledge.

The ledge was all rock and it was slanting so no one could stand on it without taking a chance. Between the cracks in the rock were small bushes growing.

I said, "Get down on your hands and knees, quick. Don't try to stand there."

Now that he was down there on the ledge I saw how risky it was. Before there was any one down there it didn't seem so very dangerous, but as soon as I saw a person on it then I was sorry I had let him do it. I didn't see how he was going to look over the edge because he'd have to keep his hands toward the wall to hang on. He'd be taking an awful chance if he faced the other way.

"It's pretty slanting, hey?" Westy said.

I said, "Don't trust to it, hang onto the bushes."

"I'm all right," Warde said.

"No, you're not either," Hunt told him; "we can see how it is from up here better than you can. Do you slip? Look out!"

"I'm all right," Warde said.

"Only don't get reckless," I said. "What's the use of taking chances? I'm sorry you went down. If you can stand up maybe I can reach you."

"What do you mean, reach me?" he said. "What do you suppose I came down here for?"

"You're pretty game," Westy said, "but look out."

By that time Warde was on his hands and knees. He was keeping hold of the stuff that grew through the cracks and letting himself out toward the edge of the shelf. We all stood at the top watching him and we were pretty anxious.

I said, "Don't turn around, go backward."

"How am I going to see anything that way?" he called. "Whoa—a——" he said, and just then he let go one little clump of bush and grabbed another. It gave me the shudders.

"That was coming up," he said.

I called to him, "Warde, don't try to turn around on that ledge. Crawl back and see if you can stand up enough so I can get hold of your hand. We'll call the whole thing off."

He didn't pay any attention to me, but moved around so his head was toward the edge. About three feet more and he would be able to look over. It gave me the shivers just to watch him.

Will Dawson said, "It's too late, he couldn't get back up here now."

I knew that was so—that he wouldn't be able to get within reach of our hands. If it turned out that he couldn't go all the way down I didn't know what would happen.

He was clutching little clumps of bush with his hands and sort of holding himself back that way. All of a sudden he slid forward and only stopped himself by pressing a little patch of bush between his knees. I could see he was holding his knees together with all his strength. Even still he slipped a little. I guess by that time he realized himself the danger he was in, but he didn't say anything.

Westy flung off his coat and threw it down, keeping hold of one sleeve. He called, "Here, grab hold of that with one hand if you can."

"I can't let go," Warde called.

His back was toward us so he couldn't see the jacket, but the rest of us saw that it wasn't within his reach. When Westy threw it, it went maybe within two feet of Warde's hand and then fell dangling against the cliff.

"Let's tie two jackets together by the sleeves," Hunt said.

"He wouldn't dare let go to catch hold of it," I told him. "Can't you see he's hanging on with both hands and feet now? He can't afford to take any more chances; it's bad enough already."

"Watch your step, don't move," Westy called down. "If you've got a firm hold hang on; don't try to look over. Give us a chance to think."

Warde called, "Wait till I see how it is below and maybe you won't have to bother to think. Maybe I can go down all right."

"That fellow's game," Westy said.

"Safety first," I called. "You're in a pretty bad place, Warde. You can see better how it is up here. You hang on with both hands and feet and give us a chance to think. Don't get excited. We don't care anything about the hike now."

"All right, go on home," he called. "I'm going to see whether we can climb down here or not."

"He'll make a scout," Dorry said.

"If he lives to take the oath," Westy said.

All of a sudden Warde moved. I don't know whether he slid or moved on purpose. Anyway there was a little clump of bush in his hand. He threw it away and clutched the ground in another place. That brought his head to the edge of the shelf. Jiminies, my heart was just pounding in my throat. The palms of my hands were all wet, even. None of us spoke. One more move and he'd be over the edge. I wanted to call and ask him how it was below, but I sort of felt that even my voice might start him moving again. He was way out of reach of us now, right on the very edge, and we knew that his life depended on how the land was below him. Because one thing sure, he couldn't come back.

Just then he slipped ever so little and I could see his knees and feet pressing the weeds between them tight, just as if his legs were a vice. I just couldn't call and ask him how the land was down there.

Pretty soon he spoke. His voice sounded just the same as usual even though it was a kind of death sentence he was saying.

"It's straight up and down," he said.

"How far?" I called. My own voice sounded strange to me.

"'Bout seventy or eighty feet," he said; "maybe a hundred. I can't tell exactly."

Then he seemed to move again but maybe I only thought so because I was so excited.

"Hang on," I said. That was all I could say.

"I will," he said. "But so long, if I don't see you again."

CHAPTER XXIX
THE LAST HOPE

"Hang on and don't move," one of the fellows called to him. "The hike is off. You just hang on. You haven't got another inch to move in. Don't look around even." I don't know who it was that called, all I know is it was one of us.

"What can we do?" I said.

Westy said, "Let's take off our stockings and tie them together."

"Good idea," Hunt said. "Look — he's moving again."

"Don't get excited," I said; "he didn't move. Hurry up, all of you, take your stockings off. Are you all right?" I called to Warde.

"Guess so," he said.

"Don't look down, it'll only get you rattled," I said.

"What do you mean — rattled?" he called.

I said, "Well, can't you take a little advice? When you're in the scouts you'll learn that you can always hang on tighter with your eyes shut."

We took off our stockings and tied them together but there was so much space needed for the knots that they made a line only about five feet long. So we tied a couple of our scout shirts on by the sleeves. Then Westy took hold of one end and I took hold of the other, and we pulled. It pulled out in one place and we fastened it again. It was a clumsy kind of a line and we didn't know whether it would hold or not. But it was the only thing we could think of.

Then I called to Warde, "Don't move till we tell you. Are you slipping?"

"Guess not," he said.

"Don't move even if you feel something on your back. We're going to throw a line right near your hand."

I grabbed the end stocking and wound it around my hand so it wouldn't slip away. Then I threw the other end, the end with the shirts. It went over the edge of the shelf within about three feet of Warde's arm.

"Don't grab it yet," I said. "Wait. Don't let go."

I began pulling to make sure the line was strong. Maybe the shirt on the end was caught on something below the shelf. Maybe the line would have held Warde all right if he moved back on his hands and knees. But anyway, it didn't hold when I pulled on it. I guess I pulled too hard. Anyway the line broke right near my hand and most of it went over the edge of the shelf.

"There it is at the bottom," Warde said. He didn't seem excited or disappointed. I never saw a fellow like Warde Hollister—never. I've seen brave fellows but never a fellow just like him.

"It wasn't your fault," Westy said; "what next?"

I guess Warde must have heard that because he called, "Nobody's to blame. You tell my people."

I was nearly crying. I said, "Warde, you hold on. You're not slipping, are you?"

"N—not much," he said.

"Don't trust to those weeds," Westy called. "Can't you get your fingers in a crack or a crevice or something and brace yourself back? We'll take off every stitch we have on and make another——"

"I'm slipping, fellows," he said. "I was a scout anyway, hey? No, I wasn't——"

"You're the best scout that ever was, Warde," I called to him. I was nearly crying, I couldn't help it. "Only hang on—please hang on—do you hear? Please hang on. The bushes—just wait——"

By that time the fellows were all undressing. Poor Pee-wee was so excited and nervous he just tore his shirt off.

"It's too late," Warde said—awful calm. "I'm slipping. These blamed weeds don't hold. Don't you fellows worry. Maybe I'll land — —"

We could see well enough that his head and shoulders were over the edge. It was just a case of one root coming up and his grabbing another one, and slipping a little each time. In about another half a minute he'd have only his legs to hold on with. I haven't got much use for lifelines made of old clothes. They're all right in stories but where there are a lot of knots fastening together different kinds of clothes, one knot is pretty sure to give way. The only kind of line we could make now was a pretty clumsy kind of a one and it would take us at least ten minutes to get it made.

By that time Warde would be....

CHAPTER XXX
A GOOD TURN

"There isn't time to do this," Westy said.

"Well, we'll do it whether there's time or not," I shot back at him. "Hustle, all of you, get your clothes off. There's time until he disappears. Two of you fellows follow the hill north and go down at the nearest place you can get down. There isn't any bee-line now. No, don't you go, Pee-wee — Dorry and Will go. Here, take my scarf, you've got your own, too — never mind looking at the tree," I said. "Here, take this shirt, too. You know how to stop blood flowing, don't you? Put a stick under the bandage and wind it round. Hurry up, he's slipping. We can't get this blamed thing ready in time. Do what you can for him down there. Hurry...."

It was funny, but as soon as they started I just couldn't help looking over there to the ridge at that big tree that had guided us all day. Kind of, I wondered if it knew the trouble we were in — and that after all we wouldn't get there. But I only thought of it for about a second.

Down there on the ledge Warde was almost half over. He couldn't use his hands to hold on with now, but he just squeezed the bushes between his feet. He was slipping over slowly.

"Hang on," I shouted; "we're hustling, we'll throw you a line."

"Look, look!" one of the fellows who had just started away shouted. "Oh, look!"

I just clapped my hands over my eyes for a moment; I couldn't look. I just couldn't. I knew what it meant. My hand was trembling and my heart was just choking me. "Did you — did you hear him — land?" I asked.

"Over there — east," some one said.

I looked in the direction we had come from, and as sure as I'm writing this, there was some one running pell-mell right toward us. I saw right away it was a girl. You know how a girl runs, especially when she runs fast. She was holding her head way back and laughing, and her hair was all flying loose. There was something big and kind of gray colored around her neck—very big and clumsy. I stood just about a second, then I made a sprint for her. I never ran so fast in my life. We came toward each other just flying. Her cheeks were all flushed and her hair was all over her face and she was panting and laughing all at once.

She said, "I—I—I—I've—got—your—rope—so there. I—I—ran all—the way—with it. You—you said—I—I—I——"

"Don't talk, give me the rope!" I said.

"Maybe—I—I—fooled you about—about the house—my own—house—but I can do things too—run—see? Here. They caught—the bandit—here——"

I ran pell-mell back to the edge with the rope. "Did he—did he go over?" I called.

"Hurry!" they shouted.

Gee, I wish you could have been there to see all that. There were the scouts of my patrol, all half dressed, jumping up and down and yelling, "Hurry, hurry!" There was Dora Dane Daring coming along behind me and all the scouts cheering her. I can hardly tell you just how everything happened. Westy grabbed the rope from me and by the time I looked over the edge, all panting and trembling, there it was right over the edge of the slanting shelf.

But Warde Hollister wasn't there!

CHAPTER XXXI
TOMBOY

For about five seconds my blood ran cold. I kind of seemed to see everything just as if I were dreaming. Then I noticed that all the fellows were hanging on to the rope. And I saw that Will and Dorry hadn't gone away. I saw that the rope was tight, down over the edge of the hill and across and over the edge of the shelf. I knew that Warde Hollister must be hanging on to the end of that rope. He wasn't trusting his life to any old weeds now. That rope was held by scouts and he should worry. And we should worry, too, because by that time we knew Warde and we knew he wouldn't let go.

I just jumped up and down shouting, "Hurrah, hurrah!" I couldn't help it. It seemed awful funny for seven fellows to be holding one up, but Warde had come so near to death that I guess they wanted to make saving him double sure. Even Pee-wee was tugging on the rope with both hands, his cheeks all puffed out. The girl just stood there panting and laughing.

She said, "What's on the other end of that rope? An elephant?"

I just went right up to her and I said, "Dora Dane Daring, on the other end of that rope is the best scout in the western hemispheres, including Flatbush and Hoboken — the best scout with one exception, and that exception is you."

She said, "Oh, isn't it just too funny to see that little Pee-wee pulling on the rope? Oh, dear! I could just kiss him. I'd run two miles to see that!"

I said, "Tell me——"

"You finish before I tell you anything," she said. "Did I save the bee-line hike?"

"Did you!" I said. "You saved a fellow's life too. You're going to get a hero medal if I have to go over to National Headquarters and see Mr. National personally. Meanwhile you can kiss Pee-wee six times if you want to."

"Look over the edge and see if the rope is chafing, Roy," Westy said to me.

"I'll do more than that," I said. "I'll go down there and stuff a jacket under it. Give me a jacket, somebody." I was feeling so happy I didn't care what I said or did.

The fellows got beside a tree so that the rope went part way around the trunk. That way they could pass it out easily. We were sure of the rope, that was one thing.Hemp—you've got to go some to break that. That was no clothesline. Backyard ropes are all right, but not for scouts.

"Don't take any chances," Westy said. "Just look and see if it's chafing on the edge."

"If it is, tell me," Pee-wee puffed out.

"Let it down slowly," Warde called. "What are you waiting for? It's all right down here."

There were only two places where that rope could rub; those were on the top of the wall right near us and down on the edge of the shelf. We knew it was all right below that on account of what Warde had said. In both of those places the rope went over clumps of bushes and moss. No rope will stand rubbing all the time, but all we had to do was to let it down to the bottom and we knew it would stand that much rubbing.

So we just passed it out little by little and pretty soon it was slack. Then we could hear Warde calling from away down below.

"All right," I shouted; "We'll be down pretty soon. Take a rest."

We tied the rope good and fast to the tree and then I said to Will and Dorry, "How far did you go when you started from here?"

"Not more than ten or twenty feet," Dorry said.

"Then the bee-line hike is saved!" I said.

Dora said, "Oh, I'm so glad. I wondered how you'd ever get down the cliff. When the men came back from Riverview Park they had that horrid bandit with them—just think!"

"What did I tell you?" Pee-wee said.

She said, "Oh, I think it was just wonderful how you fastened him there——"

"Without the loss of a single life," the kid shouted.

She said, "And when I saw that villainous creature and thought how you had really caught him, and when I saw the men had your rope, I was just stricken with remorse for the way we girls fooled you. I said, 'I'm just going to run after them and take their rope so their hike won't be spoiled.' Because I thought you'd need it. So you'll forgive me, won't you, for pretending to be so brave when all the time it was my own house? You will, won't you?"

I said, "I don't know much about the girl scouts except that they giggle a lot but I'll say this much, they know how to run and when it comes to good turns——"

"Will you let me prove I'm a scout? A real one?"

I said, "You're as real as real estate. All you have to do is say what you want."

She said, "Will you let me climb down that rope and go with you, and finish the bee-line hike with you?"

"G-o-o-d night!" I said.

107

CHAPTER XXXII
BEE-LINES AND THINGS

Gee whiz, I didn't know what to say. I didn't want to tell her that I was afraid she couldn't do it. But we had just seen one narrow escape and I didn't want her to take any chances.

I said, "If you think we're mean, we'll say yes, you can go with us. Because we owe you a lot, that's sure. I'd rather give up the whole thing than be mean about it. And I think you're just as good at doing things as we are. But we wouldn't do this ourselves if we weren't already in for it. Our clothes are all torn already from going over roofs and climbing on those ferris-wheel cars, and you'll only get your dress all torn and what's the use?"

She just stood there a few seconds, kind of trying to make up her mind. "You think I'm afraid," she said.

"I don't think you're afraid," I told her. Pee-wee started to speak and I told him to keep still. "But what's the good of taking a chance and getting your dress all torn?"

She just said, very stubborn like, "I want to go and I do think you're mean if you don't let me. I'm a scout as much as you are. You think I'm a coward. Do you think I want to go back to the village and finish a tennis tournament after seeing the things you do?" She was almost crying. I knew if she started to cry we'd have to let her go.

I said, "You claim you're a good scout and I say you're as good a one as I ever saw. You saved a scout's life by doing a good turn and I guess that's enough. But the principal thing about scouting is to finish what you begin. That's why we're here. It doesn't make any difference whether it's a hike or a dinner or a — tournament or what. If you begin it you've got to finish it. If you're a quitter you're no scout. Maybe you like to risk your life and I know you don't risk your life playing tennis. But just the same that's your bee-line hike for to-day."

"I hate tennis," she said.

I said, "Yes, but you don't hate bee-line hikes and if you're supposed to be in a tournament to-day then that's your bee-line hike. And if you don't finish your hike you're a quitter. See?"

"I'm not a quitter," she said.

"I know you're not," I told her. "So you're going back to finish the tournament and get some practice because to-morrow afternoon I'm coming over to Little Valley to beat you."

"Playing tennis?" she said.

"That's what," I told her.

"I can beat you with my left hand," she said.

"All right," I said, "I'm coming over to-morrow to find out. You go home and practice. You finish your bee-line hike and we'll finish ours and to-morrow afternoon at two o'clock − −"

"Will you be sure to be there?" she said.

"Positively guaranteed," I told her. "Good-by."

"Why don't you say 'so long' like you do to boys?" she wanted to know.

"So long, see you later," I called.

She was awful funny, that girl.

CHAPTER XXXIII
FROGS AND HATS

One by one we let ourselves down that rope. The only hard part was keeping hold where it went over the edge of the slanting shelf. The cliff was sheer up and down just like Warde had said. But that was the end of our troubles with Nature. Gee whiz, I can get along with Nature all right, but when it comes to farmers—just you wait.

We were mighty glad to see Warde all safe and sound. I said, "Warde, you're the gamest scout that ever lived, but you're reckless. If we had stopped to think we would never have let you go down on that shelf."

He said, "I'm not a scout yet, remember."

"Remember nothing," I told him. "If you keep on, and live through it, I'll have an Eagle Scout in my patrol, I can see that."

"You're never killed till you're killed," Warde said.

"You have to thank that Daring girl," I said. And then we told him all about it.

"Don't ever give up, that's the thing," Dorry said.

"Do you know who you remind me of?" Pee-wee asked Warde. We were all sitting around on the rocks at the foot of the cliff, taking a rest.

"No, who?" Warde asked him.

"A frog," the kid said.

"A frog?" I asked him.

"Sure," he said; "a frog in a story."

"I'd be pleased to meet him," Warde said.

"There were two frogs," the kid said, "and they were out for a walk, and do you know how one of them didn't get killed?"

"Break it to us gently," I said.

"They fell into a bucket of cream," the kid said.

"Was it ice cream?" Hunt asked him.

"It was rich cream," the kid said.

"It was wealthy cream," I said; "go ahead."

"They started to drown," the kid said, "and one of them got discouraged and lost his nerve and didn't try to swim any more and he was drowned."

"Very sad," Westy said.

"The other one kept swimming and swimming and kicking and kicking," the kid said, "and do you know what happened?"

"Can't imagine," Warde said.

"Just by kicking and kicking," the kid said, "he churned some of that cream into butter and pretty soon he was standing all safe on a little island of butter. So that's what he got for not giving up."

"Did he tell you that himself?" I asked him.

"You make me tired," he shouted.

Westy said, "Well, this isn't getting us up the ridge, is it? What do you say we start?"

I said to the kid, "Are you sure that was real butter, or was it just butterine? The Island of Butterine, discovered by a frog scout of the Pollywog Patrol."

"If we start jollying Pee-wee we'll never get up the ridge," one of the fellows said. So then we started.

Now from the desert island of Butterine (just under the cliff) to the ridge was maybe as much as a half a mile. For a little way the land was flat and open and then the ridge began. We would have to go up the side of the ridge. What I mean by a ridge is a long hill, oh, as much as several miles long. We knew a road ran along on the top of that ridge. For a little way we could see the big tree up there. Then, as we came closer to the ridge we couldn't see it on account of the woods.

Now the next adventure we had was before we came to the base of the ridge. I told you there were open fields and the railroad ran north and south. Until we reached the tracks we could see the tree. Pretty soon after that we had to use our compass going up through the woods on the ridge.

All along in the fields beside that railroad track were big wooden signs telling people what they should buy. The country would look better if those big signs were not there. You know the kind of signs I mean—the kind you see when you're riding in the train. One of them says everybody should want to make his home beautiful, so he should buy a certain kind of paint, because beauty is what counts. If the man that owns that sign is worrying so much about things being beautiful I should think he'd take that sign down.

One of these signs was very big and it happened to be right in our path. It says, "Brown's hats are always on top." Maybe that's a joke, kind of. We crossed the tracks and then about a hundred feet farther was the sign. There was a man there who was just finishing doing some painting on it. He had a stepladder and a can of paint and things, and he had a camera, too.

"Maybe that's Mr. Brown," the kid said.

"More likely it's Mr. Hat," I said.

Then I said, "Hey, mister, we're on a bee-line hike and we'd like to go right under that sign if you don't mind."

He said, "Under or over, suit yourselves. The world belongs to the boy scouts."

"Let's climb up the ladder and go over," Westy said.

I said, "No sooner said than stung. Over the top for us."

The man laughed; he was a good-natured man. So we all climbed up on the ladder, one after another, and while we were waiting for the man to carry it around to the back of the sign we all sat in a row on top. Right underneath us were painted the words "Always on top." I made a picture of that sign with all of us sitting on the top of it. The one in the middle is Pee-wee.

Pretty soon the man began laughing and he called up, "That's very good, all sit just where you are a minute. That puts a dash of pep into the ad. Scouts always on top, eh?"

"What's he going to do?" Pee-wee said.

"He's going to take a picture of the ad with us in it," Westy said.

I guess we must have looked pretty funny from down below; anyway the man kept laughing. The way Pee-wee sat there was enough to make any one laugh. He looked as if he thought he was famous already.

The man called, "Just sit naturally and laugh."

"That's easy," I told him; "laughing is our middle name."

"All right," he called.

Then he got behind his camera and held out his hand for us to keep still.

"What are you going to do with it?" one of us called down to him.

He said, "Well, pictures of this ad are used for all sorts of things—hat boxes, everything. Your faces will go all over the country."

"Mine?" Pee-wee shouted.

"Yes, and very likely we'll use this idea for the big signs too," the man said. "We might have some wood cut-outs for scouts. How would that be?"

"Not for this patrol," I shouted down. "We're not wooden scouts."

"Are we a part of the ad?" the kid shouted.

The man said, "That's what you are. Always on top like Brown's hats, eh? Now I'll tell you what you boys do, if you're not in too much of a hurry. You just sit up there till the next train goes by. I've got to hustle to Addison station to catch that train. Our advertising man, Mr. Bull, will be on it and he'll see just how the sign looks with you youngsters on it. I dare say he'll reward you."

"We should worry about rewards," I said. "We're part of an ad, that's enough for us. We'll sit here if the train isn't too long coming."

He said, "Well, you suit yourselves about that, but you've given me an idea and I'm much obliged to you. I think we'll use the scouts-on-top idea."

"We're like Brown's hats, hey?" Pee-wee shouted.

"That's it," the man said.

"Pee-wee's like a soft hat, he's young and tender," Hunt said.

"Sure," I said; "you're the tallest one, you're a high-hat."

Dorry grabbed the top of the sign because the breeze was blowing a little. "I hope I don't blow off like some hats," he said.

The painter went away and we all sat there singing:

"Nine little boy scouts,Asked to sit and wait.One of them got blown off,Then there were eight."

114

CHAPTER XXXIV

A LITTLE BIT OFF THE TOP

We liked that verse so much that we made another one.

"Eight little boy scouts,Glad there ain't eleven.One of them fell backward,Then there were seven."

Westy said, "If they have a row of wooden scouts up here with the words always on top underneath, that will make a good ad, hey? I wonder how much they'd pay us to sit here all the time?"

"Labor is very high," I said; "about ten feet up. Maybe they'd give us some hats."

"Everything is going up," Westy said; "let's go down."

"Wait till the train goes by," I said. "I'd like Mr. Cow to see us, or whatever his name is."

Then Westy began singing:

"Oh, boy scouts they were nineThey were sitting on a sign."

Then Dorry started,

"They do not fear a cop,They always are on top."

And then I sung out,

"They ought to cross the flats,But they're advertising hats."

Then Pee-wee started yelling,

"Oh, Mr. Bull,Your ad is fullOf scouts and bull."

"We ought to get a dollar an hour for this," Warde said.

I said, "Aren't you satisfied? Haven't we made you famous? Right away you want to pass the plate."

"You mean the hat," Westy said.

"This is the Brown's Hat Patrol," Will said. "They're superstitious, they believe in signs."

"Listen, here comes the train," somebody said.

"Sit up and look pretty," Dorry shouted.

"We've got all the signs on Broadway beaten," Hunt said.

"Sure," I said, "this is a live sign, full of pep. All sit up straight when the train passes. Remember Mr. Wild Bull is in there. Maybe he'll give us a job on a sign up on top of a building in New York. I'd like to be an electric sign, wouldn't you?"

"I'd rather be a sign of spring," Westy said.

"You'll be pushed over backwards if you crack another one like that," I told him.

"Look at Pee-wee," Dorry said.

I had to laugh at the kid. There he sat right in the middle, straight upright, with his hand up making the full scout salute as the train came along. He looked like a little radiator ornament for an automobile. I guess he felt very proud being part of an ad.

As the train went past all the passengers looked out of the windows, laughing. The more they laughed the straighter Pee-wee sat. All of a sudden, good night, over he went backwards, kerflop, into the marshy land just underneath the sign. All the people in the train howled.

He came up the ladder, with mud and grass all over him, just in time for the people in the last two cars to get a look at him. They just screamed. They even came out on the back platform of the last car, cheering him and laughing at him.

"I—I bet I sold as many as a hundred hats doing that," he said.

I said, "Good night, was that a part of the ad? You look more like an ad for bathing suits than for hats."

He climbed back into his place pulling the wet grass from his face and clothes.

"That's the time you weren't on top," I said. "I hope Mr. Wild Bull didn't see you."

"Here comes a man across the field," Dorry said.

I looked around behind me and saw a man with a great big straw hat and a shirt like a checker-board coming across the field. It seemed as if he was all shirt and hat and suspenders.

"I think there's going to be something doing," Westy said. "I can feel it in the air."

"Thank goodness, we're on top," I said.

CHAPTER XXXV
LOGIC

The man came around in front of the sign and looked up and said, "Well, now, what do you youngsters think you're doing here?"

I said, "Well, we're not so sure but we think we're sitting here."

He said, "Anybody give you permission to come on this land?"

Westy said, "No, but we know lots of people cross here and we thought it was all right. We always heard this was a short-cut to Addison."

Then he asked us if we were going to Addison.

Westy said, "No, but it's just the same crossing your land in one place as another. You can't blame us for thinking it was all right."

The man said, "Well, 'tain't right, by no manner o' means. You're trespassin', that's what you're doing."

Dorry said, "We're sorry."

The man said, "Well, so'm I, because I'm goin' to make an example of you, that's what I'm goin' to do. I'm goin' to learn you a lesson."

I said, "No lessons, this is vacation."

He said, "Haow?"

Westy said, "We're sorry, we can't do any more than say that. We thought it was all right. I don't see what harm we do."

"Well, you'll find out," the man said, good and cross.

All of a sudden Pee-wee shouted down at him, "Anyway, we're not on your land, we're on this sign. Has the sign got a right here?"

The man said, "Well, you youngsters, the people that pay me to let this sign stand here don't pay me to let you climb all over it. Now you come down off there, every one of you, and we'll see what's what. We'll see what the jedge has to say."

"Don't go down," Dorry whispered.

"That shows how much you know about law," Pee-wee shouted down. "My uncle's got a friend who's a lawyer. If this sign has a right here we have a right here because we're part of the sign. You can, ask Mr. Bull who works for Brown's Hats if we're not. Do you see what it says on this sign? Always on top? That means us. It means us just as much as the hats. We belong here, so there."

The man said, "Haow did you get here without trespassin'?"

I said, "That isn't the question. We're here because we're here. The question is has the sign got a right to be here?"

"Sure," Pee-wee yelled down, "that's logic." He looked awful funny sitting up there and shouting down at the man. "Suppose a thing has a right to be in a place but the people that own that thing don't own the place. If you're on the thing — —"

"You ain't got no right there," the man shouted up.

"Lift the ladder up," Westy said.

"Sure, that's strategy," Pee-wee said.

So we hauled the ladder up out of the man's reach.

"Do you admit that somebody can own a place that has a thing on it that belongs to somebody else that has something on it — —"

"Shut up," I said. Then I said to the man, "It says on this sign that we're on top. You see it? That means us. This kid is right; we're part of this sign, just as if we were painted here."

"Put that ladder down," the man shouted.

"Does it belong to you?" Westy said.

"It's on my land," the man hollered at us.

I said, "Well, we just took it off your land."

"If you want to take the sign away go ahead and do it," Westy said.

"We should worry," I called down.

"We can stand on the law, can't we?" the kid piped up.

"We can sit on the sign, that's better," I said.

The man said, "Are you going to put that ladder down here?"

"No, we're not," Westy said.

"We're part of this sign and we're going to stay here," the kid said. "If anybody paid you money for letting the sign be here, that includes us. We're an advertisement of Brown's Hats, that's what we are. We're on top. It says so. If a thing belongs to a thing, it belongs to that thing and not the land that thing is on, doesn't it? If you rent out a place to put a thing then the thing that's on that thing isn't trespassing on the land that was rented out for the thing underneath it, is it?"

"It's as clear as mud," I said. "We've got as much right here as a man's hat has got on top of his head even if his head is in the wrong place."

"That's logic," the kid shouted.

"It's as true as a false alarm," Westy said.

"Truer," Warde put in.

"A sign is something that's got something on it," our young hero shouted. "Let's hear you deny that."

"And it doesn't make any difference what's on it," Dorry said. "An ad's an ad, isn't it?"

"Most always," I said. "It says here we're on top, so there's the proof. We're here because we're here. You can do that by long division."

"We're secure," the kid said.

"As long as we don't fall over backwards," I told him.

"Anyway, we're not trespassing now," Hunt put in.

"Posilutely not," I said.

The man said, "All right, if you've got a right there, stay there. Only don't come down on my land. If you've got a right on top, you haven't got any right down here. I'll let you see some logic, whatever that is. You can set up there and I'll set down here, and you can stay till the sign rots. You're such clever youngsters. Always on top, huh? Well, you can stay up there with Brown's hats and see how you like it. This land down here belongs to me, by gum!"

CHAPTER XXXVI
THE SIEGE

He sat down on a nice big comfortable rock and took out a pipe and filled it and started smoking. He looked as if he was going to stay there for a couple of years or so.

Will Dawson said, "Now you see what we get for standing on our rights. About ten years from now our skeletons will be found sitting on this sign."

"Always on top," Westy said.

"If we go down there we get arrested; if we stay up here we starve," Hunt said.

"Sure, that's logic," I said. "I'm not so crazy about being part of an ad."

"We've got a right here, it's a technicality," the kid said.

"Yes, but I'm not so stuck on technicalities," I told him. "You can't eat them."

"Let's drown our sorrows in song," Westy said.

So then we all started singing and this is what we worked around to:

"We're here because we're here,Deny it if you dare;And the reason we're up here,Is because we're not down there."

I said, "Believe me, I've had enough of the advertising business. I'm getting hungry. The next time I pose it will be for a restaurant."

"I'm going to retire from the hat business," Tom Warner said. "See where it's left us."

I said, "Sure, we've risen very high in the hat business. We've risen to the top. How about our bee-line hike?"

"We can go through everything except a jail," Westy said.

The farmer just sat there on the rock with one knee over the other, smoking his pipe, very calm like.

I said, "I wonder if we could go to sleep here like birds?"

"Pee-wee ought to be able to," Westy said.

"Sure, he's a canary — —"

"Will you keep still with that?" the kid yelled.

"I wish the weekly animated news of all the world could see us now," I said. "'Boy Scouts marooned on an ad,' that's what they'd put. 'Starving on a desert advertising sign.'"

The farmer down there on the rock didn't laugh at all, he just sat there smoking.

"This is a siege," the kid said.

"We're blockaded," another one shouted.

"I bet Minerva Skybrow could get us out of this," I said. "Anybody who likes algebra — —Hey, Scout Harris, I thought you said that a scout is resourceful. Can't you pass out a little resourcefulness? We'll turn into mummies up here."

"We'll sacrifice our lives for Brown's hats," Warde said.

So then we started to sing again, each scout singing something different, but pretty soon we all got in line with this; it's a kind of a sequel to "Over There":

"Way up here,Way up here;Just our luck,To be stuck;Way up here.And we won't go home,'Cause we're stuck away up here."

"Oh, here comes the painter!" one of the fellows shouted.

"Shaved!" I yelled.

"He was shaved before," Hunt said.

"I mean saved," I told him.

"He has reinforcements with him," Pee-wee shouted.

"There's one of Brown's hats with a man under it," Ralph Warner said.

I said, "I guess that's Mr. Wild Bull. Thank goodness, they'll relieve the starving population."

"Anyway, we held out," the kid said.

"Sure," I said. "The battle of Brown's hat sign. Wounded, none. Killed, none. Hungry, everybody."

Then we all set up a cheer for the painter and the other man. When they came near enough I shouted, "Hey, mister, we're thinking of retiring from the hat business."

"Hey, mister," Pee-wee shouted; "aren't we a part of this sign?"

"Absolutely," the painter said. "You're the best part of it."

"Now you see!" Pee-wee shouted down at the farmer, "You thought we were just hanging around here. Now you see! We're just as much on top as the hats are."

"Except when we fall down," I said.

"A man's hat might blow off, mightn't it?" the kid yelled. "That wouldn't prove his hat isn't on top, would it?"

"That's a very fine argument," the man who was with the painter said.

"I know some better ones than that," Pee-wee yelled down at him. "Do you know we caught a bandit?"

"Hey, mister," I said, "haven't we got a right up here?"

"That's what it says," the man laughed.

Then the painter said, "Boys, I want you to meet Mr. Slinger Bull, advertising man for Brown's hats. He is very much taken with the idea of having scouts on top of our signs."

I said, "Believe me, we came near being taken. We're going to retire from the business."

Mr. Bull said, "Too late, your pictures will soon be all over the country."

124

"Mine too?" Pee-wee yelled.

"And we're going to use the scout idea—scouts on top; wood cut-outs, of course."

"Wouldn't live cut-ups do?" I asked him. "Because that's us."

Mr. Bull, he just laughed and he said, "Who's leader here?"

"I am," I told him.

He said, "Well, I want your name and address. We'll probably want you to pose. Did you ever pose?"

Pee-wee said, "We were in the movies, in the imitated news."

"Sure, we used to pose for animal crackers," I said.

"Hey, Mr. Bull," Dorry called down; "if we're on this sign are we trespassing?"

"No more than the paint is," Mr. Bull said, looking kind of sideways at the farmer. I guess Mr. Bull saw how it was all right. "You boys are protected by your contract with Mr. Grabberberry here. You're absolutely safe, you're covered."

"By Brown's hats," Westy said.

Mr. Bull said, "Exactly. The sentence above refers to you. You've given us an idea."

"We have lots of ideas," Pee-wee said.

I said, "I've got an idea we'd like to get away from here; we're hungry. We've been in the hat business for over an hour. We've got a date with a tree."

He said, "The world belongs to the boy scouts. Everybody knows them and likes them. To say they're on top is just telling the truth. I think we will hook you boys up with Brown's hats. We may ask you to pose. Brown's hats are known the world over. Step right down, boys, and have no fear."

"Did you see me from the train?" Pee-wee asked him. "Did you see me fall backwards? I bet I sold a lot of hats that way, hey?"

"Oceans of them," Mr. Bull said.

You can bet we weren't afraid with a bull to protect us. We went down the ladder and the farmer didn't say a word. I guess he was thinking about the money he got from Brown's hats all right. He said to Mr. Bull, very nice and polite, "I kinder thought they wuz trespassin', you know. 'N I was a-scared they'd get inter some trouble."

"Believe me," I said, "we can't get into trouble because we never got out of it. Anyway, we like the hat business pretty well and I wouldn't mind living on a sign except for getting hungry."

So then Mr. Slinger Bull tried to make us take five dollars for our trouble, but we wouldn't take it because scouts don't accept money for that kind of a service. Anyway, it wasn't a service at all, it was just fun. I bet you never heard of anybody being marooned on a desert signboard before.

CHAPTER THE LAST
(THANK GOODNESS)
IT HASN'T GOT ANY NAME

Now that was the last adventure that we had that day. But we've had a lot since then. We picked our way up through the woods on the side of the ridge, using our compass, because we couldn't see far ahead. It was getting dark and the woods were awful still. Every time a twig cracked under us it seemed to make a loud noise. There were crickets chirping too. It kind of reminded me of Temple Camp after supper. We kept straight west because we knew that was where the tree was. I guess we all got sort of excited as we came up near to the top of the ridge.

I said, "I'm glad the last part of our hike is through the woods. Maybe we had a lot of fun in Bridgeboro and in Little Valley, but the woods for me."

Pretty soon we came out into the open and there in the dusk stood the great big tree all by itself. It seemed awful solemn like.

Westy said, "Look! Away off there in the east. See?"

Oh, boy! Away, way, way off across the country we had come through was like a shaft of dust sticking right up into the sky. It was the searchlight on the Bridgeboro fire-house.

"Let's start a good big fire," I said, "so our folks will know we're all right. Then we'll start home."

So we started a fire and sat around it and jollied each other and especially Pee-wee—you know how we're always doing. And we roasted the potatoes that we had with us and they tasted good, kind of like smoke.

After a while Westy said, "Well, here's the end of our bee-line hike and I bet we didn't go more than about ten or twenty feet out of our path all the way."

"That's the only way to get any fun out of a bee-line hike," I said. "Either do it right or not at all."

After we were all rested and had eaten all our potatoes we trampled the fire out and went up to the stateroad about a quarter of a mile away to wait for the jitney. I was good and tired, I know that.

Warde said, "I've been sitting on the porch all summer reading adventures, but this beats them all. And the best part is it was all real."

"Believe me," I told him, "a real agate is an imitation compared to us."

"I'm glad I'm in the scouts," he said.

"The worst is yet to come," I told him.

He said, "I'm game."

"You bet you are!" all the fellows shouted.

We all looked back and said, "Good night, old tree, see you later." It seemed as if that big tree had been with us all day and we had come to be friends, sort of. Maybe it saw everything from up there and was laughing to itself at all the crazy things we did, hey?

As we went along toward the stateroad Dorry said, "Let's take a hike straight north to-morrow."

"Sure, for the North Pole," Hunt said.

"You can count me out," I told them. "I'm going over to Little Valley to-morrow to play tennis if anybody should ask you."

Right away that crazy kid started jumping up and down, shouting, "What I know about you! What I know about you!"

I should worry about that bunch. Believe me, I was glad to think of getting rid of them for a day.

So long, I'll see you later.

THE END

129

Milton Keynes UK
Ingram Content Group UK Ltd.
UKHW010728130923
428592UK00004B/178